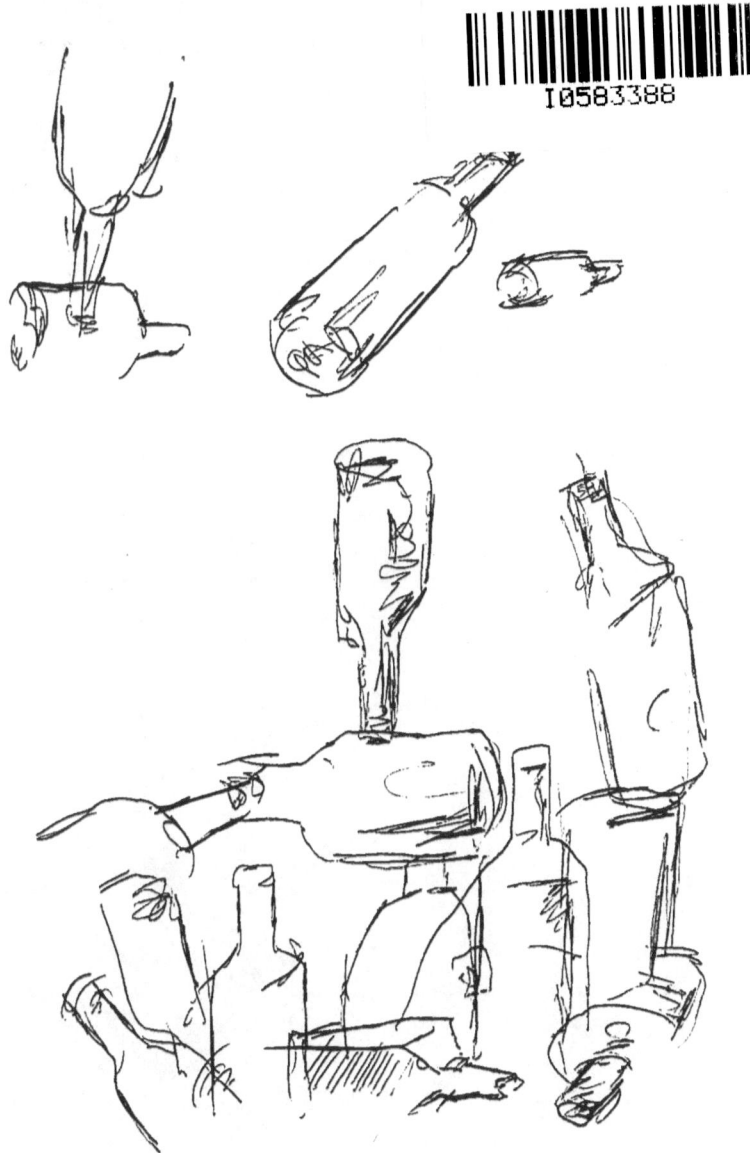

—Why are you drinking? the little prince asked.

—In order to forget, replied the drunkard.

—To forget what? inquired the little prince, who was already feeling sorry for him.

—To forget that I am ashamed, the drunkard confessed, hanging his head.

—Ashamed of what? asked the little prince who wanted to help him.

—Ashamed of drinking! concluded the drunkard, withdrawing into total silence.

And the little prince went away, puzzled.

Grown-ups really are very, very odd, he said to himself as he continued his journey.

—Antoine de Saint-Exupéry, *The Little Prince*

ISBN-13: 979-8-9926281-3-5

This is fiction but I didn't have to make anything up.

Paperback edition of a theoretically infinite number

Printed aboard the Death Star by underpaid hourly workers

Typeset in Janson and Smith Corona Silent

Written, drawn, and designed by Dmitry Samarov

Published by Pictures & Blather in Chicago, IL

dmitrysamarov.com

OLD STYLE

Dmitry Samarov

Pictures &Blather

Ah! well a-day! what evil looks
Had I from old and young!
Instead of the cross, the Albatross
About my neck was hung.

—Samuel Coleridge

also by Dmitry Samarov

All Hack
Soviet Stamps
Music to My Eyes
Making Pictures is How I Talk to the World

PRICES

Flyover

It's not how it used to be. It never was.

The Western Flyover goes down quick. Built to ease traffic around Riverview Park, it has in recent times become a run-down eyesore. The park—where so many Chicago children rode roller coasters, ate cotton candy, went on first dates—

bulldozed and gone fifty years when the wreckers come for the overpass.

I watch the machines whacking away at the concrete of the pockmarked bridge until the rebar sticks out all over like frayed nerve endings. A small crowd gathers to gawk. A fat man shimmies up a nearby lightpole and furiously snaps photos.

I stand back a bit, closer to the Marathon station where American United Taxi used to be. In a year this gas station will be gone. The building across the street where the Chicago Dispatcher cabbie newspaper and the Point diner were is now an empty lot behind a chain-link fence.

As each structure disappears, bits of my history follow. What remains is mutable, growing fuzzier every time I remember. With no buildings as proof, the time I spent in them feels made up.

The Blue Light is a corner bar in the middle of a block.

The Old Style sign swinging at all hours against the whipping wind doesn't say ZIMNE PIWO like so many around Chicago. Just BLUE LIGHT. The bar stands where the northern end of the overpass used to be. A typical Chicago two-story building with an apartment upstairs and a business street level.

After 9/11 the jukebox was full of America-will-put-a-boot-in-your-ass songs. But they would've been on there even if the Twin Towers still stood.

The Blue Light was a dump. The kind of place where promotional Budweiser ads hang dusty and fraying decades after the beer reps dropped them off. Years after what they advertised is no longer on the market. These posters were the decor because the owners didn't care about what their bar looked like and because they were free.

But the day I watch the overpass come down, the Blue Light is no longer *that* Blue Light. There is now a big picture window and exposed brick walls inside. The bar is along the north wall of the room rather than the south the way it was in my day. Also, many flatscreen TVs. Peering in, it's clear it's been out of business for some time. I haven't been inside since long before Sharon and Kenny sold it. I think back a few years to when I dropped off a couple here in my cab. They were fighting the whole way. She started flirting with me, asking if I'd park the cab and go in with her. She was doing it to piss off her boyfriend, but it came off as a perfect example of what the Blue Light had always been: a dark place where men and women go to treat each other badly. I did my best to soothe the guy's ego as I let the couple out into the oversized mitts of the gorilla guarding the door. This was definitely not my Blue Light. Sharon and Kenny were way too cheap to hire a bouncer.

—I got lead in my pencil but no one to write to.

The punchline to Wes's favorite Viagra joke. He tells it every time. I'm happy to pretend to laugh because it's one of the few in Wes's repertoire without the word *nigger*.

Wes is built like a fire hydrant. A squat bald man who fancies himself a real cut-up. He's a doorman at a big apartment building. When he isn't bitching about the rich people who live there, he's ragging on his coworkers—all worthless niggers, according to Wes. A couple hours and a dozen Miller Lites in he gets weepy, asks if I ever met Gayle—his dead ex-wife.

Wes is my favorite regular at the Blue Light.

***

I turn away from the bar's darkened façade and look where the overpass used to end. I can see across Western Avenue now to the sprawling cop station on the other side. When I worked here, I'd listen for car and motorcycle engines idling, then cutting out, as regulars parked underneath the ramp.

I see Timmy the Cabbie's American United Crown Vic left angled sideways while every other car is perpendicular to the roadway. He's inside trying to mooch a dollar stein of Old Style off Wes or Bill or one of the others. Timmy's face is scuffed and scratched like he'd used it to screech to a halt outside the bar to save the cab's brakes.

I see Bill's behemoth Harley. Tassels, detailing, storage racks and all. Hard to believe it never collapsed under that mountain of a man after he walked out of the bar, a case of Miller Lite augmenting his prodigious gut.

Sue's out there, her SUV idling as she talks on her cell. She's still in her Wrigley garb. She'll run inside in a minute or two, breathless, ready to get behind the bar, or sit and drink with her girlfriends if it's her night off.

Tommy used to sleep in the underpass sometimes. I see him out there near closing time, waiting to come in to mop the floors in exchange for bottomless Old Style. Tommy was the first one I got to know at the Blue Light after Sharon.

I see the shithead I cut off earlier in the night loitering in the shadows, waiting for me to come out after I've thrown away the empties. Does he have a gun? A knife? A bunch of his deadbeat pals posse'ed up to kick my ass?

***

I knew about Riverview Park long before I got to Chicago. I read about it in a book. It's where Lefty Bicek takes Steffi on their date, before leaving her in a basement to get gang-raped by guys he's known all his life.

Now there's a cop station and a strip mall where the park used to be. Cops came into the Blue Light and put their service weapons on the bar before ordering frosty mugs of Old Style. I wonder if they kept coming once it changed hands and the flatscreen TVs were installed. I have no idea what kind of bar it became, but doubt it was one where it was okay to put a gun down next to your drink.

All that was twenty years ago. Now I work at another bar across town.

My life is totally different.

ABC Bartending School

I had no in, so I did what suckers do: I signed up for a class advertised in the *Reader* next to massages and unwanted household goods. Had to borrow $200 from my folks to pay tuition.

The ABC Bartending School is above a liquor store in a lonely building in the West Loop. A makeshift classroom holds tables covered with bottles of yellow, red, orange, blue, pink, and green water and different glassware. Twenty students take turns making Pink Squirrels, Harvey Wallbangers, Fuzzy Navels, Sex on the Beaches, Kir Royales, and dozens of other cocktails we'll never make if we land an actual bartending gig.

Our instructor is a tired-looking old fellow. He goes through the motions. What landed him at this sorry place is likely the same thing that landed his students here. No clear direction. No prospects. No way to pay for what we do because we have to. Bills due but the current gig is killing our insides. A half-hearted Hail Mary.

The ad in the paper promised an income of hundreds of dollars a night and job placement upon graduation. After pouring many dozen ersatz forgotten drinks into brandy snifters, cordial glasses, flutes, and Collins tumblers, we're given a diploma and a hotline number updated every Friday morning.

For the next month I sit by the phone Fridays as 10 a.m. approaches, fingers ready to dial. The first half dozen listings never change: pizza chain, suburban hotel bar, Tex-Mex joint, you get the idea. I don't have the heart to try them. I know I can't handle a place with a uniform or a corporate employee manual. I'm too old for flair. I keep hoping for some neighborhood spot. A mom-and-pop.

Sharon's message gives little description of her bar, but I call anyway. She answers as if I'd interrupted something important. Like she's running very late. We set a time to meet.

The Blue Light, with its standard-issue Old Style sign waving slowly in the wind, looks like every other Chicago tavern I've passed without a second look. Each has a crowd for whom it is a home away from home, but if it isn't yours, it's indistinguishable from the one down the street or miles across town. Through the diamond porthole in the front door, I see a rail-thin woman with curly brown hair and eyes popping out of her head running around a fiber-board-paneled bar decorated with peeling beer ads and neon signs. I push the door open and introduce myself.

After confirming I graduated from the bartending school, Sharon launches straight into training. I'm hired.

She shows me the gray lockbox under the bar filled with cash for poker machine payouts, stressing in no uncertain terms not to pay out to anyone I don't know. Strangers are to be told the games are "for amusement only" like the stickers next to the screens of spinning slots say. Every other bar along that stretch of Western Avenue gets raided. The Two-Way, a few doors down, closes for good after they get busted. But the Blue Light is spared. So many of the regulars are cops and you don't shit where you eat.

She shows me what to set the pizza toaster oven to and how the popcorn popper works. She tells me to add fifty cents to all drink prices after 2 a.m.—a kind of unhappy hour premium. Most of the bar's business is transacted in those two unhappy hours.

I never ask Sharon about where the bar's name came from. Did she and Kenny name it or inherit it from the previous owner? The Old Style sign swaying in the whipping wind above the door, likely from the '70s or before, hints at the latter.

Was it named after the 1932 Leni Riefenstahl film?

Or maybe after Cherenkov radiation—the phenomenon responsible for the blue glow in nuclear reactors.

More likely it's a tribute to the sprawling police station across Western Avenue. As one cop put it, "Blue isn't the greatest color for visual perception, but it works just fine for things that really matter."

Genre Scene

Dutch tavern scenes color the way I think a bar should look. Dark, earth-toned rooms with light from small windows barely illuminating carousing patrons. This faint sideways light obscures as much as it reveals. Yet these unkempt places are often the center of the community.

Children squat over chamberpots, dogs jump up on tabletops for scraps, and men and women recede to remote corners to get to know one another better.

Beer is tapped directly from giant wooden casks and poured into steins, sloshing and spilling over the floor as drinkers dance and jostle. It's a merry disquieting scene. Are they happily celebrating or drowning sorrows? What's the difference?

Steen, Brouwer, and van Ostade painted their pictures to document the life of their cities. I want to do the same. But is there any remnant of the wild abandon of 17th-century Holland in 21st-century Chicago? If I squint and ignore the firefly glow of cellphones—replace them with candlelight or kerosene—I can see the rudiments of a classic tavern scene while sitting against the back wall of the Albatross. The heavy wooden beams buttressing the ceiling, the clusters of talkers and revelers, the hum of inebriated blather, it's not so different from an inn in Leyden.

What I love in a bar is that people are both in public and not. We see one another but break off into smaller groups, forming private bubbles where we forget about others who can still see and hear what we're doing. Behind the bar I'm often just the deliverer of drinks rather than a fully-fledged person. It gains me access in ways unavailable to those on the public side of the bar. They forget I'm even there between orders. As long as their glasses are full, conversation is flowing, or whatever's occupying their attention on phone screens isn't disrupted, they're oblivious and let their guard down.

They don't know or care that anyone is watching or listening.

What am I hoping to catch? Some clue as to what it's all about. A true moment when a person says or does what they mean rather than performing for others. I get glimpses, but only when they're sure no one is looking.

It's this same thing I remember from the Dutch paintings. Half-lit vignettes in a larger tapestry whose edges disappear into darkness. Every group and solitary figure doing life's dance. This humble scene repeats every day in many places over centuries.

We stop once we can no longer dance.

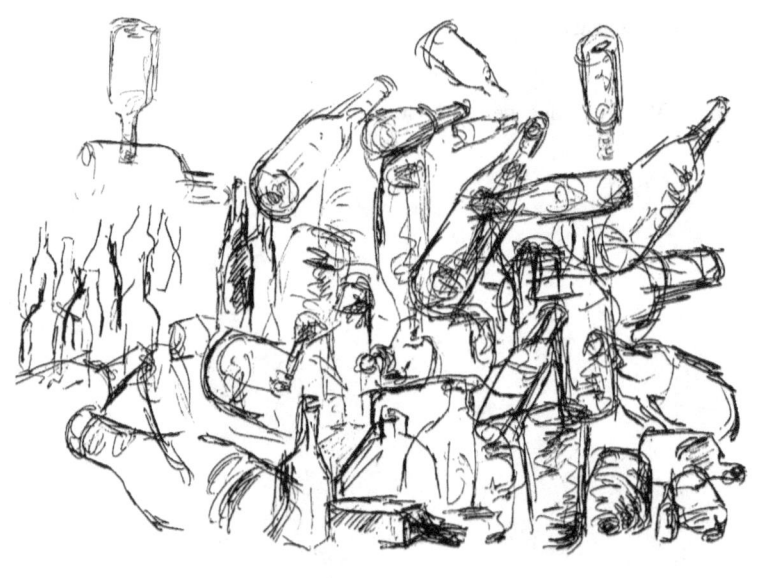

The Golden Years

There are no Tom Waits tunes on the Blue Light jukebox. It's not how the regulars here see themselves. Toby Keith, Kid Rock, Charlie Daniels, Ted Nugent. Dwight Yoakam is as edgy as it gets. Few true troubadours of the bottle to be found. They want to sing along rather than cry. But what do they have to be so happy about?

I never drank less than the year I worked at the Blue Light. That might sound odd, counterintuitive. For eight hours a night, three, four nights a week, I had an endless supply of booze within reach but rarely took a sip. The people are the reason.

Watching Blue Light patrons get pickled is like a *Scared Straight* ad. Each has their own tipping point, but once cleared, they're a broken record. Wes gets weepy over Gayle, Candy screams at Junior, Hillbilly slams through the door already in a rage. They do the same thing like clockwork. Then come back the next day and do it again. I sit and watch the horror show. I politely turn down the shots they offer. It's a way for them to feel closer to me. It's an offer of friendship.

But I don't want to be their friend.

Sue sings along to "Where Have All the Cowboys Gone" because she really wants to know. There are no cowboys at the Blue Light, though plenty wear boots and hats. It's only a look. None will be roping any steers or riding the prairie. The closest most will come is chain-smoking Marlboro Reds. But the bar allows them to look the part. The blurrier vision becomes, the more likely that squinting at the stranger a few seats away will make him appear a hero.

I had my times drinking when I was a kid. I used to take a bottle of Jack to matinee movies, then go drive cab twelve hours, sometimes stopping off at bars along the way. But I never wanted to do much more than soften the edges. I was never trying to nullify or forget.

Nostalgia's built into boozing. At the Blue Light, they try to drink enough to summon the past. Whatever their banner year, the way back lies via Old Style and Jäger, Ice House and Fireball, Pabst and Cuervo, Lite and Beam. Once there, they reminisce. The faraway look comes easy once they're cross-eyed. They don't like that I won't join them, but they forget about me before I even walk away. The golden years beckon, and if I don't come along it's my loss.

When I look back, I want to forget.

Across the bar they think what they see with their eyes is ugly. They think there was a better time. When they were younger, prettier, stronger. When the chicks were falling all over them. They see it clear as day after a few rounds. I look at them and see gin blossoms, wrinkles, discoloration, loose skin. I don't see them the way they see themselves. I'm only interested in how they are, not how they were, or might've been. Maybe it's a lack of imagination.

I wonder whether Wes or Bill ever read Bukowski. I binged on his books in high school but can't recall if I found his wallowing in alky life romantic. Teenagers like extremes. I know I didn't dream of growing up to be one of his characters. There was a yuppie joint called Chinaski's down the street, but it didn't last. I bet their clientele didn't know it was named after Bukowski's alter ego. The bottom of the barrel rarely yields top dollar.

They don't see themselves as losers or failures. They come here and see familiar faces, buy each other rounds, and disappear into yesterday.

Ask for Rose

Lon pulls out an oversized scrapbook. Yellowed newspaper clippings jut out from between the pages where they've waited for decades to be pasted in. Lon starts a dozen projects a night but never completes any.

Today he's excited because he retrieved this scrapbook from the alley where Hazel left it for him or the trashman to pick up. He's happy he beat the garbage truck and rescued it. He turns and turns the pages, ads and articles raining down on the bartop like lazy snowflakes. They settle haphazardly about him. Many will remain just where they are for days, weeks, months. Then he'll happen upon one or another and become rapturous, insisting it's the exact thing he's been looking for. Then the feeling passes and the scrap settles on some other surface to be forgotten again. Some of his treasures go through the discovery/neglect cycle many times over. Each and every time they're the most important thing ever. Until they're not.

He wants to show me the ads his mother placed in the paper for barmaids, musicians, bartenders, and the like. Some go back to the 40s.

WAITRESS—White, attract. Single. For cocktail lounge, 6 nights. Easy work. Age 24-40. $1 hr.

PIANO PLAYER—Young lady. Or guitar or banjo. Play on request.

MUSICIAN—Piano-accordion. German or Lithuanian speaking. Must be good. For week-ends.

Then they change. No more cocktail waitresses or accordionists needed anymore. She's selling the bar.

TAVERN—ROSE'S ALBATROSS—Well estab. Good business. You will not be sorry if you buy this place. Widow aged, retiring.

I ask Lon when this one's from, but he doesn't know. Decades ago for sure. His father died and she tried to get rid of the place. But she's still here living a thin wall away from where we're sitting. Lon is terrified of her. They avoid each other. Communicate primarily via cellphone even though they're rarely separated by more than a few feet.

BARTENDER—Lithuanian-speaking, middle age, married to work in nice place 7 p.m. to 4 a.m. or rent to good honest man. No drinking. Must have good refs.

This is how Rose and Lon's father met. It used to be her father's tavern. He died so she took over. Jack answered her ad for a bartender. He wasn't married but filled all her other requirements. She rented him a room upstairs, down the hall from her own. He took to visiting hers after mopping up the floors and throwing away the empties around 5 am. She was eight months pregnant with Lon's older brother when they went down to city hall to make it official.

Lon's memories of Jack are hazy, rose-colored. He passed when Lon was still in high school, training to become a draftsman. He dropped out to help Rose with the bar. He has nothing bad to say about the old man but still blames him for leaving him to this fate. Running a bar in the same building he's lived all his life wasn't Lon's dream.

TAVERN FIXTURES for sale—Front and back bar, good condition, 2 yrs old. 10 ft workboard and sink with refrigerated section; beer tap; G.E. reach-in white-enameled refrig, 30"x76"x66"; barstools; tables; chairs; booths.

They're all still here. She never found a buyer. I wonder what she planned to do after getting rid of it all? She probably had dreams too. Instead she stayed. She comes out of her room sometimes after I close the bar. She looks in the coolers to make sure I restocked the bottles and cans. She opens the icemaker door and squints up inside to see if it's making ice.

If Lon is down here already, he acts put out. Like a teenager being checked on. He doesn't look her way. His answers to her questions are pissy, monosyllabic. After she disappears he launches into tirades about how she doesn't trust him to do anything. How she controls his life. You would never believe the man is pushing sixty.

WIDOW ALONE CAN'T HANDLE.

Whatever Rose needed, was missing, after Jack passed, she never got through her want ads. But she kept placing them. Some of the ones preserved in Lon's scrapbook have dates.

They range from the 40s to the 70s. What made her stop trying and retreat to the room behind the stage with the flat-screen TV?

Lon says she remarried three or four times after Jack. He doesn't tell me his stepfathers' names, whether they worked at the bar, how long they lasted. Only that Rose could turn heads well into her sixties. He admires her, loves her, but she terrifies him. He's still the little boy trying to please her. He was never her favorite. Jim, his older brother, can do no wrong in her eyes. He's a fuck-up who wrecked a motorcycle that left him with a left leg he drags around like dead weight. He rarely visits. When he does come by, he gets hammered at the bar and hits on any woman who will let him for the price of a draft beer. He's hateful to Lon. Mocks him for never leaving home. Yet expects his share from the till.

DEATH IN FAMILY FORCES SALE

There were no takers, so Lon and Rose are still here. One day they'll both be gone, but there will be no more ads in the paper about the Albatross. Nobody sells anything in the newspaper anymore. The building and all that's in it will be listed on some real-estate website. Maybe pieced out through virtual flea markets and bargain bins. The rest will be hauled away for salvage. The structure leveled to make way for glass and drywall dream homes. No one wants what Rose has been trying to sell for longer than anyone can remember.

Ghost Hooker

—Can I ask a weird question? Is this place haunted?

She came in with a big wedding party. They're all near the back of the bar by the photobooth, three tables pushed together, laughing, drinking, and taking pictures.

She wanders up to the bar by herself, steps out of sparkling high heels, leaving them on the floor by the ice machine, and plops down on a barstool. She stares through the mirror, somewhere past the liquor bottles, storage room, to the empty lot past the long-shuttered currency exchange.

She twirls an unlit cigarette between her fingers while sipping at her drink. She asks about ghosts again.

No, I say, I've never seen any. But this has been a bar for a hundred years, so unsettled spirits wouldn't be out of place.

I make a lame joke about the only spirits around here being trapped in bottles, which doesn't register with her at all. She says it's a thirteen year old boy and points at several spots around the room where she sees him. She begins to get upset that neither Eber the doorman nor I see what she sees. We reassure her that we're not mocking her.

She asks my name and says hers is Ellroy. I don't ask if her parents named her after the writer of *The Big Nowhere*. She asks where I grew up, and when I tell her Boston, she gives me a knowing look.

—Honest answer? I used to be a sex worker in Vermont. I went to Waltham, Brockton, Burlington all the time.

She tries repeatedly to maintain eye contact, gauging what effect her revelations are having.

When I come back, she's guessed Eber's sign. She nods slowly and reveals that he has a troubled relationship with his grandmother. He plays along, wanting to hear more about the thirteen year old ghost haunting our bar.

Next time I return, she looks deep into my eyes and asks how I'm doing. When I say I'm doing fine she doesn't believe me. She orders an old-fashioned.

—But don't make it too sweet. I want it extra bitter. With Bulleit Rye.

Then she asks Eber if he can score her some coke.

She says we're disrespecting the ghost by not acknowledging it.

—What's the best shot? Ok, give me a whiskey.

She takes a sip, then pushes it toward Eber and wanders outside to smoke. She wants another whiskey fifteen minutes later, but I tell her the time for shots has passed. She badgers Eber about cocaine some more.

Her fellow wedding revelers leave and she follows. Eber is disappointed when I tell him she was a prostitute. He thought when she said he was cute, she was being sincere. After I close the bar I notice her sparkly heels still sitting on the floor by the ice machine.

I leave a note for Lon about Cinderella leaving her slippers. Maybe she'll come back for them. In the meantime her thirteen year old ghost can keep watch until they're safely back on her feet.

Innocent When You Dream

Lon's a hat guy. It's not because of the bald spot. Or, not only because of it. It's his self-image. He sees himself as a doomed romantic hepcat. On open-mike nights at the Albatross he breaks out his harmonica and ukulele. "Innocent When You Dream" is his go-to. When he's done singing he talks the nearest woman onto the dance floor and holds her too close as they turn to the music in the narrow space between the barstools and the stage. They don't push him away but few stay for a second dance.

Lon once ran into Tom Waits. It was at Wise Fools Pub on the North Side. If he told me the year, I can't remember. It doesn't matter. It's become origin story and myth.

Lon was still drinking back then. It was late. Probably after Waits's gig someplace in town. Lon sees him come in and battles with himself to keep cool. Doesn't want to lose his shit in front of his hero. Asks the bartender to send Waits a shot. When it's poured, Waits looks Lon's way, nods in appreciation, then waves him over. Waits says he's off the hard stuff, sips a beer instead.

Lon gets a faraway look telling me this story. There's no

ending. But it's as if he's still there drinking with Waits as decades drag by.

Any guy in a fedora or porkpie hat and a vintage shirt is a Waits wannabe on first glance. He didn't invent or patent the look, but he's the one I think of. Most women roll their eyes when they see one of them. It's such a fallback affectation. It implies a longing for a white-bred yesterday. Not that every guy in throwback duds is a woman-hating racist, but that retro shit leaves a sour aftertaste.

In a neighborhood that used to be notorious for white hate, the Albatross is a beacon of welcome to all colors and creeds. But Lon can't rid himself completely of the bigotry of his upbringing. His people battled for their place in the new land, sometimes stepping on others to do so. The fact they were treated badly when they got here doesn't stop them from treating others the same way.

I love a lot of that old-timey shit too. Can't help it. I just can't commit to wearing period garb. Dressing like a noir extra is kind of funny. Lon doesn't really pull it off. He doesn't smoke and he quit drinking years ago. It's not period-correct if it doesn't reek of Pall Malls and rye whiskey. So what does it mean to adopt some parts of the past and discard others?

I hear we're past history now. The web makes everything from any time available at a keystroke. Is there a when anymore? If you can mix and match with no context, do any of the parts retain any of their old meaning?

Waits always knew his look was a pose. He played with it, mutated and remixed it over the years. But like Jesus, his apostles spread his gospel to the letter. It became a lifestyle with its own strict rules. It doesn't take much to start a religion. A new one's hatched every other day. Lon's saving grace is his inconsistency. He doesn't have the discipline to be a true believer.

He just wants the dream to be real because his everyday is rarely enough.

Like most insomniacs he's often half-asleep with his eyes wide open.

Can't Recall

Folly greets me at the door like a long-lost friend. Her eyes, divots in her boulder-like pitbull head, take me in as if from centuries past. Her welcome tells me I'm in the right place.

It's my second date with Callie. Fourth of July. An unbearably humid Chicago summer night. Callie's block is a war zone of fireworks. A haze hangs over the whole street. But upstairs, after I close the door, I barely notice the explosions. Or, rather, they seem muffled, as if miles away rather than directly under the window. I don't know if it's Callie's willful magic or a side effect of attraction.

***

I met Callie at a party I meant to avoid. A fundraiser for a film magazine I used to write for. I felt an obligation. Then I see her.

I'd biked past the building a million times but never been inside. A lonesome structure along an overpass, surrounded by railroad tracks—the Amtrak yard sits to the north, giving on to the Chicago skyline. The building housed some industrial concern at one time; now it's a rabbit warren of art studios, small businesses, and marginally-kosher live/work spaces. My destination is a film post-production facility.

There's a bottleneck by the door. A woman at a table is soliciting donations in exchange for raffle tickets. A group bunched up by the narrow entryway agonize over which prize to donate towards. Beyond them I can see the room filled with people. Anxiety spikes. I know I'll only last minutes. Maybe just drop a few bucks in the jar and turn around and leave? Then I see her.

She stands just beyond the donation table, next to a couch that looks like a family castoff. An old man is offering to refresh her glass of wine. She glows. Or, everyone around her appears in shadow. A light-color floral summer dress and cork-heel sandals show off toenails painted seafoam green. Dark auburn hair, likely a dye-job, takes nothing away from her beauty. Her face, once she turns my way, was stunningly asymmetrical. Almost cubist. A Modigliani come to life.

The old man returns with a plastic glass of white wine, bows, and turns to greet someone he knows. I sit down on the couch, and she sits down next to me. She asks what brings me here. Says she doesn't know why she's here, then remembers a friend had invited her. Her job is picking music for movies. I show her my sketchbook filled with drawings of people playing music. We talk when she isn't looking through the book. Her praise is effusive, outsized. Almost like she's putting me on.

Callie's friend arrives. She writes down her number, says she wants to see me again, then turns away. I walk over to where the raffle prizes are. DVDs, posters, and gift certificates for classic movies. I can't focus on any of it. I look out the window at the Chicago skyline in a daze. I sneak glances her way but don't try to meet her eye. I don't want the spell to break. I leave without talking to anyone else.

We make a date for Saturday. She wants to try a bar in my neighborhood. I agree without saying I hate the place.

***

—This isn't what I imagined, she says, looking around. The bar has a reputation as a place for cool kids but is in fact a haven for tattooed douchebags training for yuppiedom. I suggest we walk down to the Albatross. She doesn't realize it's so close. She'd taken an Uber to meet me. I'd soon learn she has absolutely no sense of direction.

Our conversation is easy, like we've known one another a long time. Because I work at the Albatross, Callie asks whether bringing her here is awkward, like inviting someone to meet family. There could be judgment, the stakes raised. I tell her I want to show her off.

She tells me about her abusive ex now in jail for trying to kill the woman he was with after her, about fetishes, about her mad love of music. Every now and then she pauses, embarrassed she's said too much. I ask her to go on. I want to know everything. She came to Chicago a few years ago, hired as a backup singer for a local hip-hop producer. When it became clear the job offer was just a chance to get in her pants, she quit and struck out on her own, eventually landing a gig scoring an indie film. Now she spends her days searching cyberspace for sounds to match images.

Walking her home from the bar. I learn her inner compass is out of whack. Though she lives a few blocks away, she insists her place is in the opposite direction from where I know it to be. After convincing her to trust me, we're at her door in minutes. We kiss goodnight. I don't remember how I get home.

***

We worry how Folly would handle the violent bursts. She cowers from time to time but seems to be holding it together.

I watch Callie cooking our dinner. We talk, drink wine,

it feels like a fairytale. The decor is just so. I can tell Callie spent a lot of time creating this enchanted place. She turns from the stove and smiles, then quickly looks away. I never want to leave.

After dinner we move to the living room. She plays records and tells me about her family. The history of mental illness. Her grandfather in Paris who changed his last name from a Russian Jewish one to the French word for *remember*. Or is it *recall*?

I take out a pad of paper and ask her to sit still. She's never posed for a painter before, says she hates every photograph taken of her. Calls herself unphotogenic. As I work I keep trying to catch her eye. Hers meet mine, then flit away like birds momentarily alighting on a branch only to fly off at the slightest gust. She looks at the charcoal when I'm done and acts flattered. She says my drawing is what she feels she looks like.

I ask if she'd been uncomfortable posing. What would make her more at ease? She suggests taking off her clothes. But only if I do the same. She goes into her bedroom. I shed all I have on before the door shuts. She returns minutes later, lies down on the floor near my chair, takes a deep breath, and opens her robe.

We lock eyes whenever I'm not looking at the drawing.

These glances last hour. I want to disappear into the point where our eyes meet. After I can't work anymore, I lay down next to her.

Callie is out of town for work the following week. We go to the movies when she gets back, then the Albatross for drinks. I talk her into the photobooth despite her insistence she never takes a good picture. I'm looking at the photostrip now. In the ones where one of us isn't blinking, we look so happy.

She wants to see my place. It's been years since a woman slept in my bed. I get new sheets, clean the bathroom, try to make my hovel habitable. I warn her I have nothing on her where homemaking is concerned. She's excited anyway.

She takes my place in with the same wonder I'd taken in hers. We drink and listen to records. Then she changes and sits in my armchair to pose for a painting. It goes wrong from the start. While we lock eyes as before, the picture is stillborn and ugly. She sneaks a look before I'm done and can't hide her disappointment. I wrestle with it another hour, then we go to bed.

She calls herself my girlfriend. We go to sleep in each other's arms.

In the morning we go to the coffeeshop for breakfast. She's distant but not unhappy. She kisses me goodbye promising to see me soon.

I never see or hear from her again.

I know she doesn't care for texts or email. After hearing nothing from her for two weeks, I decide to appeal to metaphysical forces. On a clear night, I climb onto my roof and set the cursed portrait from our last night on fire—a sacrifice to return me to Callie's good graces. It feels good to be rid of the horrible thing. It had taunted me, reminding me of failure and heartbreak. To watch it turn to dust and be blown away by a lazy breeze is a relief. But if Callie is affected by my little ritual, I never know about it.

My last text to her asks if she's alive. Crickets.

As weeks turn to months I convince myself Callie is a figment of my imagination. A fantasy conjured by a lonely man. But then the Albatross calendar comes out. The bar makes a collage of photobooth pictures to mark each passing year. There we are, caught mid-smile, close together, in love for all the world to see.

I roll a calendar into a tube, slip in a note wishing her a happy new year, and leave it on Callie's doorstep.

The Corner of Hell & Hell

I was a regular at the Albatross years before I set foot in the Blue Light. Maybe that's why I sometimes confuse the two. Things that happened in one bar slide over to the other depending on when I think of them. Pinning down the right day and time is a problem. It's always the same nighttime in a bar.

I didn't meet Shiv at the Albatross or the Blue Light, but we spent serious time in both. Apart and together. We've been tormenting each other for decades.

Shiv calls the Albatross the corner of Hell & Hell. By the time we got together, the bar had been the setting for some of her uglier scenes. Fights with boyfriends, getting cut off and kicked out. She has few good memories here. But it's my favorite bar, so she goes when I want to go.

One time she punched me outside on the sidewalk while I was having a cigarette. What were we fighting about? Why was she so mad? She's seconds from boiling over all the time. I just walked away. She showed up at my place at three in the morning crying, banging on the door. She couldn't understand why I left. I asked if she expected me to punch her back. We keep breaking up and getting back together. I lose track of how many times, but a couple of the breakups were in the cracked red vinyl booths at the Albatross.

We both act like the other is a last chance at love. Not solid ground for a thing to last. I have so many photobooth strips of us from happy times. Now she won't set foot in the place. Bad enough to have all the history. Now her ex works here. As if out of spite, that's how she thinks of it.

I watch other couples tear at each other from behind the bar. I can feel the cold silence as each stares into their own phone, a window to an imaginary world they believe better than the one their bodies are trapped in. The TV's off except for the Academy Awards and the Super Bowl, so people have to entertain themselves with conversation when not staring into the little screens in their pockets.

Shiv went to the Blue Light sometimes, but we thought we hated each other back then.

The Albatross

I once carded Harry Styles working door at the Albatross. I didn't know who he was, but he came in with a woman who looked just like him: model-thin, flowing wavy hair, polite, British passport. For hours after, minivans full of teenage girls slow-cruised by. The girls would run in, look around, ask if we had a patio or upstairs, then leave disappointed. Styles had posted something about the Albatross on Instagram.

I swore I'd never work at a bar again after the Blue Light, but here I am.

The Albatross is a corner bar on the outskirts of a neighborhood rapidly climbing tax brackets, but inside it is as it's always been. A low-key shelter for artsy weirdos. A DMZ that welcomes anti-gentrification radicals and invading yuppies alike. The newcomers know the place because *The Breakup* was filmed here. The regulars smirk, wishing they could forget.

I think of the Blue Light every time I'm walking up to the Albatross because of the apartment above the bar.

Don lived upstairs
from the Blue Light

Don lived upstairs from the Blue Light. His Brylcreemed grey hair was neatly trimmed, buzz-cut close to the ears, 50s-style. His wife had died recently, but he was keeping it together. He worked in manufacturing. Printing plant, tool-and-die shop, I never found out exactly. Don was a man of few words.

He came in every day after work. He'd order a $1 stein of Old Style and drink it in silence, then order another. Halfway through that one, he might stammer out a word or two. Few conversations with Don lasted more than a couple moments. Still, bit by bit, I got a partial picture of his life. He had cats; he missed his wife.

Then he lost his job and everything changed.

He never said why he got laid off. He didn't talk about it. Started showing up at the bar earlier in the afternoon. I could chart his disintegration from day to day. His hair went first. No more haircuts, scraggly, uncombed. Then his checked flannel shirts weren't tucked in anymore. He developed a limp.

Soon he was drifting off, eyelids drooping, slumped sideways on his barstool. A long skein of drool inching glacially toward the bartop. I hated to jostle him, seeing he was in such a bad way, but I couldn't have people sleeping at the bar. He'd rouse slowly, his reactions delayed, as if I was in fast-forward and he was at half-speed. My words didn't reach him right

away. He'd slo-mo off his stool and inch toward the door.

The last times I saw Don, his pants were soiled. He pissed himself sitting catatonic over a half-finished Old Style. His speech slurred to the point of rarely completing a phrase. He kept trying, then start over, then give up. I didn't have the heart to kick him out. Luckily, there was rarely anyone but regulars in the place when he was in.

Don didn't come in for a few days, so I started asking around. No one had seen him. Kenny went upstairs and broke down the door. Pizza boxes, newspapers, and unwashed clothes formed hills and towers in his rooms. Don lay dead on the kitchen floor, his face eaten away in places, teeth marks still visible.

The cats hadn't been fed in a week.

US Knights

Kenny was married to Sharon but didn't tell people. He didn't want people to know he owned the Blue Light. He liked to come in and act like a customer. Not much of a drinker. He liked Tequila Rose, a sickly sweet liqueur the color and consistency of Pepto-Bismol. He blew his cover by asking me to pour drinks on the house for his friends.

Kenny belonged to a motorcycle club called the US Knights. He claimed to hold a land-speed record somewhere out west. He was a runty guy with a receding hairline and a scraggly rat-tail down the back of his leather vest. While not physically imposing, there was a menace to him. Maybe it was the motorcycle club thing or my assumption that he carried weapons. There was just some backwoods unseemliness to the man.

He had property in Kentucky. I never knew what he did there, but he was gone weeks at a time, returning with cartons of Marlboros, Camels, and Kools, that he unloaded at the bar for ten-to-twenty bucks below Illinois prices. Not unlike the Blue Light poker machine policy, only trusted regulars were told about the discount smokes.

The Blue Light had a back room that was only open on busy weekends or special occasions. A small bar and two additional poker machines, half dozen small tables, but no windows. Some nights at last call, Kenny closed the door to the bar and kept the party going back there into the morning. I wasn't welcome and was thankful not to be. I threw the empties into the dumpster, counted the drawer, wiped down the bar, and locked the front door as Tommy started to mop.

My Year Sitting
Ringside to Hell

The Blue Light was a monastery year. Long before Shiv and I got together. I'd barely been on a date since art school. Audrey, Shiv's childhood friend, comes in to bitch about Bob. I never met him, but she convinces me he's ruining her life. Shiv will tell me Audrey thought I had a crush on her. Audrey thought every guy who ever met her did. When she breaks it off with Bob, Young Will starts coming around. Will will become an alcoholic writing a book on Chicago dive bars. But he doesn't give the Blue Light a chapter. Maybe he keeps it secret so that his future groupies won't know where the great author himself drinks. By the time his book is published, Will is going to meetings three times a week, far far from Chicago.

A blown up photo of Bela Lugosi as Dracula hangs warping and water-stained over the pool table like a patron saint protector. No one who comes to the Blue Light more than once is up to any good. Few even try to pretend. Maybe this isn't the end of the line, but it is a stop or two from it. What does it say about us that we choose to spend time here? Slumming it? Gaining life experience? Can any of us do better with a little effort or higher self-esteem?

Acting doomed or lost is a pose for only so long until it becomes your life. I don't drink while pouring them but maybe I should. It would make the hours go down easier. I have no glimpse of life beyond the night I'm living through. Walking by Audrey as she tears Will a new one, I don't envy him or her, but I have nothing better going. At least they have each other to torment. What have I got?

I daydream about a night when a woman comes in alone and Bela approves when the woman acts like she wants me. She stays until four and helps with the empties. We get in her car and she takes me home.

The dream rarely gets any more involved than that. The sex scenes are by the numbers—enough to distract but not enough to lose myself in. It helps me fall asleep as the sun is rising but when I wake in the afternoon, nothing has changed and nothing will.

Sue and her friends want pizza, so I pop a sausage one in the toaster oven for them, then go back to looking at Laura's ass as she bends over the pool table to line up her shot. A pitcher of Old Style, balanced on the lip near the corner pocket she aims at shudders but doesn't spill as the cue ball hits its target. Ken laughs and fills up his stein before taking his turn. Laura's another one I dream about. In that fantasy, I make her see that Ken will never want her the way she wants him and she sees that she should've been with me all along. Bela almost breaks his beatific grin when my mind strays in this direction. The smell of burning unfrozen cheese snaps me back to now.

I never tell Shiv about Laura. There's nothing to tell because we never got together but it doesn't take much to make Shiv jealous so I don't risk it. Does anyone actually want to know everything about the one they're with? White lies and not noticing are the key, or so I hear.

Lon's Mom

Lon's mother was still alive when I started at the Albatross. I'd just moved back to the neighborhood after Shiv and I failed to marry. I was starting over.

The bar's around the corner from my new place. The Academy Awards are on. The only open seat is by the window next to a disheveled old Englishman everyone calls the Professor. He keeps up a filthy play-by-play as beautiful women flicker by onscreen. The peak is a ranting endorsement of Lady Gaga's rendition of the numbers from *The Sound of Music* over Julie Andrews's originals. Then he mutters for some time about what he'd do to Gaga if he was a younger man. I'd stopped acknowledging him an hour before. I look past him and realize the bar has emptied out. I pick up my bourbon and move as far away from the Professor as I can.

Rose's TV is going when I come in to mop the bar before opening. She comes out to watch me work. Lon hardly ever talks to her in person. They yell at each other on their cellphones from adjoining rooms. She is frail, birdlike, but she's not to be trifled with. She's outlived seven husbands and three of her five children.

—Why do I bother? I can't do nothing right according to what she says.

Lon is afraid of her, but she likes me. Calls me Mr. Coffee for the ever-present steaming paper cup from the shop down the street.

After Lon sat for a portrait, his mom came over and took a long look, then told me,

—You captured the secret Lon.

She has rooms upstairs over the bar but prefers to spend her time lying on a day bed watching soaps and gameshows on a flatscreen in a little room off the kitchen, just behind the back wall of the bar. She rarely emerges during bar hours anymore but keeps up with how the place is run. She's spent over fifty years in this building, starting as a barmaid when her father ran the bar. The cracked bits of mosaic in the doorway hint the tavern started as a tied house for one of the local breweries. Something starting with a 'B' ending in 'Brothers'. This building has housed a bar for a hundred years.

Every now and then, an old timer will come in and claim he used to come here when it was a Mexican transvestite hangout. They go on and on reminiscing about it. I don't burst their bubble by telling them they're thinking of the place across the street that was demolished decades ago. No bartender worth his salt breaks a drinker's reverie.

Lon never told me when it became the Albatross.

According to Merriam-Webster:

ALBATROSS

a : something that causes persistent deep concern
  or anxiety
b : something that greatly hinders accomplishment

If Lon had any of that in mind, he never let on. Somebody in his family probably just liked seabirds. They're just a dream to someone who's lived his whole life in Chicago.

Lon

—Tending tonight?

Lon asks while making bloody marys. Yes, I am. But he knows this. He's the one who hired me.

I'm the only one at the Albatross besides Lon. Stacks of empties are teetering by the door to the back, which means he hasn't had time to clean up from Saturday night. He probably hasn't slept. If I go through the kitchen to the back porch, I'll see a small mountain of white twist-tied garbage bags filled with crumpled PBR cans waiting to be taken through the garage and piled up by the Chinese neighbor's trash across the alley. He takes the cans to the recycling place. He always smiles and waves when he sees me throwing empties into the dumpster.

Lon has made a cardboard barrier. Behind it he cuts up summer sausage, pickles, cubes of cheddar, cherry tomatoes, and celery for skewers. On my side of the barrier, a stack of half-opened bills, drawing paper, shopping circulars, pens, markers, half-empty Monster energy drinks, and other flotsam takes a couple seats' worth of bar space. It is a remnant of what Lon starts to spread across every available surface once the doors of his bar are locked at 3 a.m. He works on his drawings, digs through bills, writes up to-do lists, and makes stop-motion animations on his phone. He puts a cot out but rarely uses it till long after daybreak. He doesn't like sleeping in his own bed, just like his mother. He goes to Cermak for bloody mary supplies, then comes back and pushes all his night projects toward the back of the bar to make room for the day drinkers.

Dozens of boxes of this and that end up in the garage. I spend months back there organizing it. I move mountains of Lon's crap from one end of that former horse stable to the other, and just when I start getting somewhere he makes me stop. He says it's because he can't pay me anymore, but he hardly payed me anyway. It has to be something else. Maybe if everything is put away, there's nothing to hide behind anymore.

One time I banged on the locked door for fifteen minutes and called his cell over and over when I was supposed to clean the bar. Nothing. A couple days later, he tells me he hadn't slept for a couple days and finally crashed. Dead to the world.

Lon asks me to cover his afternoon shift. He goes out to run errands, and there is nobody in the place for an hour or two. I start daydreaming about buying the place. What would I get rid of and what would I keep? The walls are covered with Lon's artwork, old photographs, beer ads, neons, street signs, and friends' art, Oddfellows banners. I'd dim the lights and take out the TVs. The formica bar top that Lon installed himself to replace the rotted wooden one seen in old snapshots from when his father, John, ran the place, would go too. The dolls, tin toys, figurines, and bric-a-brac that populate every spare crevice of the back bar, beer cooler, and cash register would stay. But how much could I take out and keep the Albatross the Albatross? Because I would only want to run it if it was this place, not some random bar. But would it be the same run by anyone but Lon?

The daydream dissipates. I go back to not wanting to own anything.

Oddfellows

Everyone asks about the banners above the bar. I tell them it's secret society stuff. Then they want to know if the Albatross is one of its meeting places. They get spooked and excited, but I let them down by explaining that Lon found the banners at an estate sale. They point their phones up and snap pictures anyway.

FRIENDSHIP LOVE TRUTH. That's what the interlocking rings on the banners supposedly stand for. All-seeing eyes, skull-and-bones, bundles of sticks, and other icons and logos are stitched in asymmetrical patterns. But what it boils down to—as I say to anyone who asks—is that these are flags to clubhouses for men to hide from their wives.

Lost Weekend

I see the old man on the bus home from the Golden Nugget. He's on the southbound #49 when I get on. Usually gets off at the Blue Line. Every time I see him, I think of Ray Milland in *Lost Weekend*. I make up stories about him.

His skin is sallow and he has rheumy, far-away eyes. The clothes he wears are sometimes in clashing patterns, always many decades old. This is what Don Birnam would look like if he'd waited twenty, thirty years to go for the cure. Years lost, but still alive, trying to pick up the pieces. To pin down when it all went wrong.

One time he had an accordion file full of documents. He settled into his seat, then started pulling papers out, examining this or that one with a magnifying glass. Had he come from court? At 5 a.m. on a Wednesday? Is he some kind of detective? Another time he had a worn, sun-faded box with a long-obsolete computer advertised on it. Was he going to try the internet after his typewriter finally gave out?

I've never seen him smile or talk to anyone. He looks preoccupied and bereft, like he keeps seeing it all slipping away. But I'm making that up. I don't know anything about him. I'll never ask him anything, I know that much. I wonder if anyone else on the bus notices him or thinks he's unusual.

They're in their own worlds. I keep looking and wondering if he's some kind of spirit from the past or a harbinger of the future. Like he's visible only to me to deliver a message. But what could it be? The stories I make up about him never resolve, never end.

A few days ago, on my way to the Blue Light on the #49, Lost Weekend has a fur hat on with ear warmers underneath.

He could be a minor member of the Politburo gone to seed. It's a cold day. His coat and scarf aren't frayed but look past their prime anyway. It's the way he always looks. He has a smudged blue laptop bag. He's upgraded his technology again. I can see the flicker of a handsome young man in a business suit strolling confidently toward a bright future. But that was long ago. How did it all go wrong? Where is he going now? Is there still time to make it right? To salvage some of what might've been?

It's a hopeful ending for Birnam because he's in a movie and movies call for happy endings. My guy on the bus is not onscreen.

What's his true story?

As I sit and wonder, the bus squeezes to the right of a long line of backed-up cars and guns it along the curb. Approaching Milwaukee, we hear a loud thud and see the right-side rearview mirror fly off after it clips a light pole. That slows the bus down a bit. The driver announces this will be his last stop a few seconds later.

Lost Weekend gathers his belongings with a sigh and disembarks with the rest of us. I don't know where he's headed, but I walk up Western to the Blue Light.

The Golden Nugget

At 4:30 or 5:00 am. I'm not ready to go home and sleep, so instead of catching the bus south, I walk the half-mile to the Golden Nugget. I sit down just as the *Sun-Times* truck pulls up with the early-morning paper. I can smell the drying ink as I flip to the back for the box scores and light an American Spirit.

Every waitress here knows to bring me two glasses of water along with coffee to save multiple trips. I get the country-fried steak, eggs, and grits and check to see how the Sox did the night before.

Four or five cups of coffee and as many cigarettes later, I'm through all the sections of the paper I want to read. The sun is coming out, so it's time to catch the bus home to sleep.

These vampire hours make me feel out of step with the nine-to-five world. I'm always going home just when they're heading to work. They only come into the Blue Light over the weekend when they don't have to get up the next morning. I don't even know what a weekend is. My days off are Tuesdays or Wednesdays. The work weeks never feel like they have an end or a beginning, only pauses, stops, and starts.

The waitresses at the Golden Nugget are like me. They deal with odd people at off hours. Their mornings are night-time, and the middle of the day is the time to sleep. We know nothing about circadian rhythms or pretend not to. What good is it knowing about something we can't apply to our own day-to-day.

A couple of the waitresses come to the Blue Light some-times. One has taken a shine to me. She's got a hungry look when she looks my way. She sucks down Long Island after Long Island, complaining about the father of her daughter the whole time. If this is her way of flirting, it has the opposite effect.

I avoid the Golden Nugget for weeks at a time to keep from running into her. This is one of the pitfalls of working when most of the world is asleep. You meet other night owls and some of them want to take you home with them. They think because you're both awake that it's meant to be.

Freebie

Every fifth beer is free at the Blue Light. Sharon tells me that my first day. A few regulars can hit the bonus two, three times a sitting. Bill Cash gets four or five on the house every time.

Cash is a mountain of a man. He parks his Harley by the underpass a couple times a week. Once settled at his spot by the window, he starts a Marlboro Red and orders his first Miller Lite. He doesn't talk much, which suits both of us fine. There's no animosity like with some of them. He respects my silence, while sucking down bottles in two, three gulps.

Cash works for Johnson Controls managing heating and cooling in a downtown skyscraper. He talks about the job if there's someone in the bar he knows but is mostly content to be alone with his thoughts. His demeanor barely changes from the fifth drink to the twentieth. Then, responding to some inner signal, he gathers his things, leaves a $20 on the bar, and ambles out to saddle his Harley.

Cash is a vet. One of many who come here. Another works the afternoon shift at Shoes Tavern in Lincoln Park. First time I served him, I made the mistake of putting a straw in his glass of whiskey. He plucked it out and threw it down the bar, explained he couldn't take straws since having to drink through a trach after getting injured in 'Nam.

I've rarely used a straw since.

Mom & Dad

Sharon's parents rarely see each other. They split years ago but still make snide remarks; the claw marks have yet to heal.

Mom's appearances are never announced. The door opens and she drags in cases of soda or bags of limes. Sharon makes her run errands. Eyes darting about, questioning this and that, her nervous flitting about makes me feel like I've done something wrong and she's about to find out.

Her main job is to watch Sharon's kid. The bar serves as their play area—the little girl runs up and down the line of barstools, followed by Grandma's watchful eyes. She asks about her former husband. Every innocuous remark bites, yet she can't let go, can't stop caring about his comings and goings.

Dad opens up at 7 a.m. five mornings a week but shows up when I'm closing, hours early for his shift. His left side, paralyzed by stroke, drags dead weight behind the right. The few hardened souses he serves are in no hurry and hardly move about, so it's not a problem.

Ashtrays up and down the bar hold his abandoned butts, Marlboro 100s gamely flickering and pluming before dying out. His limp left hand holds a lit one while he works the buttons of the poker machine with the right, ash collecting on the linoleum below before being scattered by the readjustment of the barstool's legs or the wheezing efforts of the overworked fan.

He bitches about her from time to time.

—That woman's crazy, always sticking her nose where it

don't belong, glad to be rid of her, he says.

Then he turns back to the spinning cherries, grapes, and dollar signs. Hoping beyond hope for the big score like every addict. Knowing all the while that every penny he wins will be fed back into the machine.

D-E-A-D L-O-V-E

A young woman carrying a heavy oversized duffel bag walks into the Albatross, takes the barstool next to mine and orders an Old Style. The World Series is on. I ask if she cares about baseball. She doesn't. Tells me she's packed for a trip to Nashville with a guy she's been seeing a couple months. They're leaving early the next morning, but he's not answering his phone. She waited at the Starbucks down the street for two hours, then came in here to drink and worry. He's never pulled anything like this before. Just yesterday he told her about all the things he wanted to do once they get there. He booked an Airbnb and a car. She was excited.

She's from Aurora and I say,

—You're from Wayne's World, and she says that everyone says that and rolls her eyes. She's been couch-surfing since summer while cocktail-waitressing at a Lincoln Park nightclub and apprenticing at a Rogers Park tattoo shop. She shows me her knuckles, which spell out D-E-A-D L-O-V-E. Says she did them herself. I tell her that it's a bit fatalistic for a twenty-two-year-old. Then she tells me about the guy she moved down to Tampa to live with. At first everything was good, but then he started getting jealous, and before long he was knocking her around. She didn't understand what had changed. Now this new guy, who had seemed so normal, has pulled a disappearing act on her.

She keeps texting her girlfriend to come out and get drunk with her. I buy her a beer and tell her this night will be a funny story one day even if it really sucks right this moment. She's not sure whether to believe me, but it gets her to smile.

She convinces her friend to come meet her at some other bar, thanks me for listening, says she'll see me around.

Candy & Junior

—My name is.

—My name is.

—My name is.

She repeats it until I say Candy. After that:

—The most important thing you need to know is.

—The most important thing you need to know is.

—The most important thing you need to know is PAY
ATTENTION.

Her husband, Junior, doesn't say a word. Just sits and nurses his whiskey. It's Saturday afternoon. After going through her routine, Candy rips into Junior. What a worthless piece of shit he is. How he doesn't love her. Then she's weeping. He tries to comfort her, but she's inconsolable. Slurring her words, looking around for someone else who will sympathize. She blubbers at me for awhile. Three drinks in, I cut her off. She doesn't understand. Stares into middle distance. I retreat to the end of the bar and light an American Spirit.

Junior puts a couple dollars in the jukebox and sings along with Randy Travis, whom he favors a little. Candy tries to sing along with "Where Have All the Cowboys Gone?" making it sound like a personal indictment of her husband.

I can't make out her words too well by the time she asks again for her fourth drink. I tell her she's had enough, walk to the other end of the bar and light another cigarette. Candy and Junior are the only ones in the bar, so I sit down on the barstool by the ashtray and open my book.

Inspector Maigret is halfway to solving the crime when I look their way again. Junior is staring abstractedly at some imaginary point along the row of bottles on the back bar. Candy's head is resting sideways on her forearms. She looks like she's asleep. I go over to wake her up.

She asks for another drink and acts shocked when I refuse. Junior argues for getting his drink whether I serve her or not. They stay there like that for another half hour while I read and chain-smoke, paying them no mind. Then they make a big show of gathering their belongings and walk out without saying goodbye.

It goes this way every Saturday.

Sunburn

I come in on a Sunday and Lon says,

—This is the result of falling asleep on top of the garage in the sun.

It takes a few seconds for my eyes to adjust to the dark of the Albatross, but now I see his forehead, neck, and chest are all an angry red. He foists his leg up and pulls up his pant leg and says,

—This is no sunburn. More like somebody attacking my leg with needles and knives.

I tell him I always forget that you get burned even when sitting in shade or when it's overcast. He says,

—It's even worse when it's overcast because it's through water or something. At least that's what I heard.

Inventory

Lon asks me to make an inventory of all the beer and booze we serve. Says it's time to raise prices. I start with the beer stored in the basement. To get there, I open a trap door in the kitchen. When the door is open, Rose can't get to the stove or sink. Lon puts a chair before the opening so she doesn't fall in. Down the wooden steps, there's a shelf overflowing with napkins, plastic cups, and other paper goods, most covered in years-old dust, unused and likely never to be used. The ceiling is too low for me to stand upright without getting hit in the head with pipes and support beams, so I crouch. Turning right, boxes and other crap are piled all the way back to the north wall. Some hold Christmas and Halloween decorations from decades ago. Lon uses some, neglects most, so they wait here.

A series of pull-strings light bare bulbs as I move east, the length of the basement. A washer and dryer, an industrial sink, glassware, unused and retired beer neons fill the rest of the space along the narrow path back to the cases of beer.

When deliveries come, they feed the cases of beer through a coal chute that opens to the street. It's just big enough for one case to slip through. I spend an hour moving cases of Okocim, Bud, Corona, Fat Tire, MGD, Old Style, and PBR from one pallet to another so they're not just piled pell-mell like they were and likely have been since before Lon took over the bar from his mother. I load a handcart with stock needed upstairs and wheel it the length of the basement, back to the opening in the kitchen floor. Because of the low ceiling and many pipes, I can only carry one case up the stairs at a time. Crouching and pouring sweat, I lug them upstairs.

The liquor on the back bar is arranged at random. Whiskey next to vodka next to tequila. Lon returns bottles to any vacated spot after pouring a drink. No prices on any bottle. When I ask how much he charges, Lon asks how much he should charge. He acts like he doesn't know even though he's the only one who decides.

The list I make includes beer and booze Lon aims to buy but hasn't yet, as well as that which he plans to phase out. About half reflects what is actually on the shelves. We raise prices on a few things but keep most the same. I print it up two-sided on a piece of cardstock and bring it in. Lon is thrilled but the sheet is soon buried in a pile of papers next to the register, never to be seen again. I print another and put it in a plastic menu sleeve and hang it on the side panel of the back bar.

No one other than me looks at it ever again.

Out Back

Behind the Albatross is a former horse stable that could hold six to eight cars when empty. It's anything but empty. The metal door is locked with two padlocks. I push it open and prop it ajar with a milk crate. I flip the switches on two sets of fluorescents hung near the wooden beam rafters and take in the sheer amount of material the building holds. Boxes, furniture, and bric-a-brac reach the fifteen-foot ceiling in spots. Guitars, bicycles, and neon signs hang from hooks up above.

Every cardboard box, plastic bag, sagging suitcase, and bowed metal shelf in the garage holds something Lon loved when he first saw it. What happened after, when he put it back here, is anyone's guess. Whether most of these objects are forgotten after decades of lying in this place or are just biding their time for when he looks at them again and remembers why they caught his eye no one knows. Lon least of all.

Crates filled with toy train tracks form leaning towers stretching upward to the rafters; sagging, decades-old cardboard boxes hold paperwork, photographs, tchotchkes, and tools; rusting tin signs and dust-covered neons advertise beers long forgotten and years out of circulation; stacks of gilded frames lean against canvases depicting creepy clowns or barely started, abandoned student art assignments; speed racks, spill mats, cocktail napkins, and glassware, all sealed and unused sit waiting on shelves, buried under layers of ceiling debris.

Every time I go in, I find something.

A collection like this takes time to assemble. Along with discarded and discounted goods are personal writings, children's doodles, and keepsakes going back over fifty years. On the one hand, this is just a room full of stuff; on the other, it is a historical record of a family's life and how it was lived. It's a great privilege to be allowed to comb through someone else's belongings. It is also much easier for a stranger, who has no sentimental attachments. Were these my boxes of past, each opened cardboard flap might send me down a rabbithole and sidetrack me from the task for minutes or hours, but because these things are someone else's I can categorize them coldly, for the most part.

A box full of matchbooks I open is like a history of the neighborhood. There's a set of six naked beauties who advertised the tavern back in the 60s and 70s, while others promote restaurants and stores so long gone that even the buildings that housed them were demolished decades ago. I'm no professional picker so I don't know how much of this stuff is truly treasure, but I have no doubt that a good lot of it can be turned over for a profit. The question is whether the man who has amassed it is willing to part with any of it.

I spend weeks pushing boxes and furniture around wondering about what it means to want to gather things for decades in this way. Each new discovery must represent a need fulfilled, and all of them together are a buffer against some inner lack or emptiness. There's no way not to feel the sadness in this room. All these things should've filled the void but by being piled back here abandoned have obviously failed. Still, picking up a matchbook or dusting off an old beer neon, I can feel a bit of the charge of possibility they each contain.

When it's all is sorted and organized in a couple months, I'll gain a measure of peace. When I go back into the garage, everything else disappears. The raping swindler holding our country hostage can't get in and neither can any other global or personal misfortune. I'm already dreading when this job will be done.

I try to bring order to the place. Dragging like things toward like things, giving each grouping its own area, widening the path through so my arms and legs are no longer scraped by sharp corners or avalanched by a wobbly tower of treasures while dragging trash back to the dumpsters. But Lon runs out of money to pay me and stops letting me go back there, even when I propose splitting profits from sales of items he's willing to part with rather than paying me hourly. He still owes me $400 from when he was asking me to keep track. I don't expect to ever see that money and don't care. I feel worse that I can't finish the job. He had such big dreams for it. It was going be a studio and a gallery to have art shows for all his friends.

Now it has reverted to wilderness much like it was before I'd started. Piles of new finds fastening onto the old like kudzu, forming an endless unnavigable landscape in every direction. A tiny path is barely discernible past walls of beer case empties where only a few weeks ago it was a wide thoroughfare.

Lon's treasure trove is a pigsty once again.

The Taxi Dispatcher

Eric weighs an easy four hundred pounds. Most weekday afternoons he pulls a chair up to one of the video slot machines, orders a Diet Coke, and whiles time away looking for a jackpot.

As hours crawl by, Eric rises only to relieve himself or to cash out his winnings, immediately feeding them back into the machine. I bring him another Diet every once in a while. He never says much except for a short greeting and farewell. He doesn't look like he likes his life much. He slumps forward, edging closer and closer to the flickering, spinning screen in front of him, the only movement that of his fingers urging the cherries, plums, and dollar bills to align in his favor.

He's a dispatcher with American United Taxi, which has offices a block and a half south on Western. The rare times that others come in during his sessions, they always greet him warmly. But I never talk to him about the cab business. He doesn't know I used to drive.

Eric dies of heart failure shortly before I leave the Blue Light. I start to drive for American United a couple years later but forget about Eric. I mostly forget about the Blue Light as well.

Theatrical Release

A mustachioed man in a trench-coat, scarf, and hat comes in. He goes up and orders a drink, then makes a show of hanging his hat and coat on the coat rack by the door. He sidles up to several groups of drinkers, chatting with them as if they're lifelong friends catching up after not seeing one another for awhile. When not talking, he twirls about the room with an enchant-ed smile on his face. Whatever play he imagines himself to be in, he's must be the star.

On his way out the door, he introduces himself as John and welcomes me to the Albatross, as if he's the mayor of the bar. On hearing my name, his smile widens further and he asks if I'm Greek JUST LIKE HIM! The fact I'm not doesn't dampen his spirits as he disappears into the night. After he's gone, I go up to Lon and ask if he knows the guy. Lon says he's never seen the man before in his life.

The Two-timers

The man wears his Red Sox cap backwards. He's in his fifties with a full head of white hair (unless the cap he never takes off is hiding a bald spot.) He's got a bit of a Leslie Nielsen/ Steve Martin thing going on—one of those silver fox assholes. And he is definitely an asshole. The woman is a few years younger. In her forties. Too much eyeliner and a lot of cleavage showing. She's a little thicker around the middle than she probably was a few years ago, but she's still an attractive woman. I don't know either of their names, but they

both know mine.

They drink the same thing: vodka/soda with both lemon and lime. With most drinkers I can gauge their pace after a round. Not these two. All I need to do is turn my head and walk away to hear him calling after me for another. She waits till I've brought him his to order hers, ensuring I have to make another trip down to the other end of the bar. This goes on for hours.

I never catch any particulars of their conversation, but the tone is often tense. Body language indicates she's unhappy with him. But most of their visits aren't spent drinking or talking. What they do is paw at each other. This isn't cute nightcap kissing. She's usually off her barstool, between his open legs, sometimes on his lap. Couples groping each other in public is rarely pretty. It's not sexy like it is in the movies. I want to look away and pretend they're not doing it.

I wait till they've disengaged to check on their drinks, walk away, then inevitably hear,

—DMITRY! Another?

I just have to turn away. It works like a charm.

Eber thinks they're having an affair and meet in bars where

nobody knows them. There's a covert feel to the way they are with each other. Like they wouldn't want anybody they know to know they're together.

But I'm speculating. For all I know, they might be a bored married couple who spice up their love life by pretending to have an affair and groping each other in public. What I know is that they don't tip most of the time, even after drinking for hours. One time, after I'd brought her drink, I reach for the stack of bills in front of him to extract $4 for it, he starts screaming,

—WHOA, CHIEF!

like I'm robbing him. I have to explain calmly that I hadn't charged her yet. That shuts him up, but he doesn't apologize for raising his voice.

Sometimes I see her at Cermak shopping for groceries with her children. She never meets my eye when I look her way.

Pretends I'm a stranger.

Sue

I work with Sue on Friday nights at the Blue Light when there's a crowd. Hair dyed blond and permed to curl, brows plucked and painted, she comes in after parking her Chevy SUV in the underpass. Cheerful and inquisitive, a wiz at small-talk, she's a natural, the kind a dive bar needs to keep the gloom at bay.

Sue's day job is pouring beer to the Wrigley faithful. Oftentimes, she blows in in full Cub regalia to unwind at the poker machine for a bit after an afternoon game. Working at the park doesn't make her bleed Cubby blue. She tells stories of overserved oafs and general assholery. She works there because it's nearby. The Blue Light is her place to cut loose, so even behind the bar it's more time off than punching the clock.

She's been in the neighborhood all her life. She raised her kids here and knows almost everyone who abuses their liver at the Blue Light. She likes to sing along when the jukebox plays "Where Have All the Cowboys Gone?"

She has a thing for one of the cops. An old guy with a drooping grey mustache. Some nights they're in the corner kissing and groping sloppily. But most of the time he treats her like a stranger. She hides the hurt in a way that shows she's an old hand at their dance.

She always bursts through the door the next day, as if nothing had happened.

Unkissed

As Alina and I talk, sitting on barstools closest to the window at the Albatross, she leans in closer and closer. The first few times she came in with her boyfriend, but he spent all his time talking to his male friends about baseball so she was bored. She started to chat up the bartenders. Now she comes in by herself all the time.

One time, the two of us go for tacos down the street. I ask where the boyfriend is and she says she doesn't know. They live together so I find this hard to believe. I ask again and this time she says he's off with his friends. Says he prefers the company of men. I ask why they're together, and she has no good answer. Mumbles something about comfort and not wanting to hurt his feelings. But she's so starved for attention. Why else invite a bartender you met a few weeks ago to lunch?

Now Alina's face is inches from mine. She closes her eyes and puckers her lips, fully expecting to be kissed. But the kiss doesn't come. I remind her,

—You have a boyfriend. Where is he? Why isn't he kissing you. She ignores my words, asks why I won't kiss her. Acts hurt. She's a sad drunk. The beers make her weepy. I look away, trying to decide what to do.

She keeps trying. Doesn't understand why I won't. I give up and leave. She never comes in again. I walk by her building on the way to the bar. Look up at her window. I've never been up there, but she told me which window it is. I wonder how she is. Whether she broke up with the boyfriend. If she still lives here, with him or alone.

On lonely nights after the bar is closed, I look at her number in my phone and start typing a message. Then I erase it. I want to say I'll kiss her now if she still wants. But I never send it.

Modern Romance

Many lovers meet at our bar.

He comes in first. A fit, baldheaded guy in his late twenties. He orders a Jack-and-Coke and asks for some quarters for the pinball machine. She comes in fifteen or twenty minutes later. A full-figured Black woman with elaborate braids. She might be his age or maybe a little older. She asks what the specials are and orders the Schlitz tallboy and a shot of Jameson. She makes a show of fumbling for her wallet until he gets the hint and pays.

From the way they greet each other, it's clear this is their first meeting. But they aren't complete strangers. This is a Tinder date. Every other single person sitting at the bar is swiping through an endless rogues gallery of romantic possibilities. These two know some curated, edited facts about one another.

Every time I pass them, they're talking sex. I don't eavesdrop long enough to get context, but one time she's going on about baby oil, the next he's talking about favorite positions, then she's saying she was in a strip club but she wasn't doing anything. They sit facing each other, away from the bar, but don't touch much. He's trying to hold her gaze, to get closer.

When it's time for another round, I forget her shot is Jameson and she makes a show of mock outrage, says generations of Irishmen are rolling over in their graves because I mistakenly offer her bourbon. I take away the Schlitz can, still three-quarters full. She asks for an Old Style. He sticks with Jack-and-Cokes, tipping about fifty cents per round but paying for all of it.

At last call she fishes out a $20 and treats him to a shot. He's trying to get her to come home with him or at least tell him where she lives. After sitting inches away from him for hours, she hasn't made up her mind. She gets up and leaves without a thank you. He follows.

Mopping

Lon first hired me to mop the floor and check IDs. He doesn't trust me with keys, so I have to bang on the door to be let in. Sometimes he crashes so hard, he can't hear me and I lose a day's pay.

Rose comes out at the smell of my coffee. I think of Tommy as I wring out the dirty water.

Tommy walks his old bike in through the door of the Blue Light, leading it like a worn-out nag. He has a winter coat on over five or six layers of shirts and sweaters year-round. He fits himself onto a barstool and waits for his stein of Old Style.

The twenty years of city life doesn't rub out the Kentucky lilt from his voice. A sound many country singers work at or over-emphasize flows freely from his wind-seared lips. He tells me his stories. Fragments about country poverty, ex-wives, and the migration north in search of greener pastures. Never a moral and rarely a point, but he always paints a vivid picture.

Stray strands of Top tobacco collect around him as afternoon turns to night. Sometimes lit butts flicker out forgotten in the ashtray after his sixth or seventh beer. He rests his elbows on the bar and stretches his back and drowses, waking occasionally to confirm that everything is as he'd left it.

He doesn't say where he lives, but odds are it's some underpass away from the wind whipping the city's streets. He turns down food with a low-key politeness.

He leaves as the late-night crowd fills the place for what

passes for a rush, returns after closing time. After I throw the empties in the dumpster, restock the beer, and wipe down the bar, he goes for the mop and bucket from the ladies' bathroom. Passing the grey threadbare mop over the chipped and worn black and red linoleum tile earns tomorrow's bottomless beer stein.

Night after day after night.

At the Albatross the mop bucket is in the ladies' room just like the Blue Light. But there are paper towels rather than a continuous cloth roll that jams and hangs greyed and twisted to the floor by the end of the night. Lon's Mom insists on plastic flowers and potpourri for the ladies' room in her bar.

I stack the barstools on the bartop and sweep butts, straws, napkins, wrappers, and shards of glass into a dustpan. Then pour hot water into the mop bucket. After I pass the mop over the length of red-and-black-tile floor, it gleams for a few minutes before drying dull and dusty. Short of ripping up the linoleum—which Lon sometimes talks about—the floor of the Albatross will never look new.

But no one who comes here is looking for new.

Barf Lie

Lon says the movies always get it wrong, but I don't know. I like Mickey Rourke pretending to be what Bukowski imagines himself to be. The Golden Horn is a lot more of a dive than the Albatross, no matter what Lon tells the college kids new to the neighborhood. Every bar sells some fantasy, but it helps if the salesman falls for his own line.

TO ALL MY FRIEEEEEENDS

Every dumb kid I know learning how to be in bars used to say it. Thirty years later, I still hear it now and then. Is that retro? Vintage? Throwback? It's rarely said with irony. But does anyone really want to be a broken down drunk like Bukowski? No romance to it once no one is paying attention.

Yuppies call the Albatross their favorite dive, then order Malört and cringe as they shoot it. They think it's funny. They're slumming but also demonstrating to their friends that they haven't lost their edge, their sense of devil-may-care. I tell the ones who bother to listen that this bar is no dive.

A dive is a bar in which the man sitting next to you has soiled himself. He drinks here because it's the only place that will have him. He needs the shots and beers to stop the shakes. It's not a happy place. The Blue Light was a dive. Happiness was in short supply there. It was an end-of-the-line joint.

Bukowski romanticized places like the Blue Light. But I got through my Bukowski phase in high school. By the time I was pouring Old Style at the Blue Light, the romance of stumble-bum holes-in-the-wall had long flickered out.

A young woman comes up and asks for a Chicago Hand-shake and I don't know what that is. She acts surprised, says it's an Old Style and a shot of Malört. I do my best not to make a face then go off to get it. When I come back she admits she's only heard it from a few customers at the bar she works at and only in the last few months. If this is some test of Chicago cred or authenticity, then I'm happy to be a phony from elsewhere.

Later there's a heated argument about whether this neighborhood is part of the *real* South Side. The city is an ever-changing amalgam of different populations coming and going. The people who claim it as theirs are usually venal and small-minded. No place should belong to anyone, especially a place as complicated and contradictory as Chicago.

A week later another drinker asks simply for a Handshake. I hesitate a moment, then get a PBR tallboy to chase her Malört. She doesn't send it back and ask for Old Style instead. Guess she's not a true Chicagoan, either. That, or the fact that PBR is a dollar cheaper and four ounces more beer, might have consoled her. Paul is at the bar, so I ask him if he's ever heard of a Chicago Handshake. He's a local historian and he's never heard of it. A quick Google search reveals the drink to be a marketing gimmick cooked up by Old Style and Malört.

If someone had asked for a Chicago Handshake at the Blue Light, they'd as likely have gotten a punch in the face as a shot and a beer. The Blue Light was no one's favorite dive because there can be no such thing. It's like saying what disease you like best. No one likes being sick. You do what you can under bad circumstances.

A dive is a place nobody wants to be.

And yet, Lon happily tells every newcomer that the Albatross is the neighborhood's favorite dive. Drives me batshit. He's trying to make the yuppies feel welcome, I know, but Jesus Christ. We've gotten into it a million times. He just won't see it my way. For a guy who's oblivious to marketing, trends, and such, Lon clings to this dive thing like a life-raft. He trumpets it like a badge of honor. Why would anyone voluntarily let their family business be called a dump and be happy about it?

If I knew the answer, perhaps I'd have my own place. But I don't know and will never be more than someone else's bartender. He can say what he wants, I know the Albatross is no dive.

The Oldest Urinal in Chicago

Last year the city's historian certified the Albatross's urinal the oldest in Chicago. He dated it to about 1910. It's a twin floor number with curving Art Deco molding up top to nominally separate neighboring urinators. But wedging oneself next to another 21st century-size male will instantly remind you that people were a lot smaller in the early 1900s. It's snug. You will certainly get to know your fellow man if you share a few moments in our historic pissoir.

It's also a popular subject of social media photography. Guys egg their female dates on to duck in and check them out, giggling like little boys. I suppose relieving oneself in the same receptacle as thousands of other men have for over a hundred years should count for something. There was talk of a city-endorsed plaque for a time, but it has yet to be installed.

The wall over the urinal has been graffittied and painted over so many times it's grown crusty. My current favorite message there is *INPEACH*. Seems like the kind of spelling mistake the president's supporters are more likely to make, but who knows? Maybe it's an admiring shoutout to his pallor.

The Cash Register

New drinkers marvel at our cash register. It sits like a monument towering over glasses and bottles on the back bar. They ask if we ever use it. After all, it's an antique. But there are bills in the drawer. No one except Lon knows how many, but they're in there.

When I started at the Albatross, Lon stressed that I should always ring up drinks. The left column of buttons goes up to $90; the right down to .00 cents. Hitting the total, the register makes a satisfying sound. The mechanical sound of gears and wheels turning and colliding, it ends with the opening of the drawer. Except at the Albatross, the drawer is never shut. That's another of Lon's rules: NEVER SHUT THE DRAWER. The key was lost decades ago, so now he has to pry it open with a screwdriver, sometimes splintering wood in the process. Bending the fittings. The register doesn't look so grand up close.

After my first few sales, I notice the register tape move in the little window and I can see the price imprinted into the paper, but there's no ink visible. I tell Lon, but he says not to worry about it. Says not to count out at the end of the night, either. Just take my hourly out, sweep up, and go home.

Throughout the night Lon comes back behind the bar and stands a moment or two at the register as if staring it down. He scoops out the twenties. He lifts the drawer to see if there are any larger bills and takes those as well. Then he disappears in the back. When I needs ones or fives or quarters he disappears back there as well.

Lon had me make up a pricelist for the bar, but I'm the only one who sticks to it. When he's working, an Old Style is a buck for the old-timers but two or three for the newbies. Women drink for free more often than not. Especially if they're drinking alone. Free rounds are sent out on a whim. When he hits the keys on the old register, it looks more like a slot machine. He pauses dramatically before slamming his finger down. Then watches the total spin to a stop in the window.

Newcomers to the neighborhood order a round, then put a credit card on the bar, ask to start a tab. I want to laugh but patiently explain we're cash only and to pay as they go. Lon has his own policies on that. Sometimes after one of his father's old friends has put in hours, slumping eventually to the point of having to be roused, Lon comes around to where they're sitting, helps them into their coats, and tells them what they owe for the night.

Few complain when I charge them more than Lon does. They know the prices at the Albatross are liable to be adjusted according to the owner's state of mind. They don't expect his employees to be as erratic and unpredictable. When he leaves to do his mysterious errands, which can last many hours, the regulars tell me stories about Lon. A few have known him since he was a little boy. They remember when he worked at the electronics store next door. The one that's now a ramen shop. He'd bring transistor radios over and take them apart at the end of the bar. He always wanted to know how everything worked. He wasn't so good at putting things back together.

Even now there are springs, gears, and dials scattered about the bar. Lon has long forgotten where they came from. I ask if I can throw them away, but he says he will use them. When? For what? He can't say. Out back he has five other cash registers in various states of disrepair. Does he think some other bar will ever want them? Most bars if they haven't switched to a POS system prefer there to be ink for their register tape. They Z out their sales after every shift. They make the bartender count out the drawer and explain voids and over-rings.

A few times a year, Lon gathers a great pile of receipts and documents, throws them in a worn leather satchel, and heads downtown to see his accountant. He tells me he's three weeks late renewing the bar license and looks worried. Says the bar may have to close a few days. When he returns, he says they somehow dodged a bullet again.

I keep ringing in drinks as if the $5s, $10s, and $12.50s are being totaled up by someone somewhere. Does Lon know how much the Albatross brings in? He pays the bills he can pay as they come in.

That satisfying sound the old register makes after adding up the charges might as well be one of those special effects from the movies.

Bill knows better than you

Bill's a little man with a big mouth. Whatever you're talking about, he knows the subject better than you. Politics, stereo components, love advice, members of your family he's never met, no matter; Bill will disabuse you of your faulty notions. Every bar has its Mr. Dooley, its Cliff Clavin. Bill's ours at the Albatross.

He's in his happy place holding forth. He'll tell you how, despite their giant eyes, owls are among the least intelligent of avian species and how the fearsome locusts of biblical plague were nothing but humble common grasshoppers and how the great song composer Cole Porter took his name from the French word colporteur—a peddler of biblical literature. There's nothing he doesn't know everything about.

On days Bill's at the bar, he arrives hours before my shift. He's a lightweight so I know he's well into his cups by the time I take over. Today he's buttonholed a young man I don't recognize. He's haranguing him about the election, inches from the man's chest, spittle flying. From time to time the guy looks around the room, over and around Bill's balding pate, which barely comes to his own chin, looking for rescue or reprieve. But none will come. Because the regulars know when Bill has fastened his grip this way, there will be no mercy. The only chance is to run for the door when Bill goes to empty his bowels, which the young man does, not even bothering to finish his drink.

Bill's gone about ten minutes. I go to the men's room to check on him and he's standing in the middle of the room, pants around his ankles, staring at the wall. I help him with his pants and position him in front of the sink, then return to the barroom.

He comes out eventually. Looking around, as if he's misplaced something, he scans the room for a familiar face, someone to talk at.

One time I sat next to him and made the mistake of revealing the model of computer I had. An hourlong lecture followed, punctuated by Bill calling me a fool. I took my drink and moved to the other end of the bar. I learned my lesson. Now, whenever he asks me anything, I agree with him. It cuts him off at the knees. He can't debate or argue, which is what he lives for. Drives him batshit. Or I play dumb. Yesterday he asked me who I planned to vote for. I ask,

—Is there an election coming up?

Today I cut him off and he doesn't argue for once. He takes forever gathering his things to go. He lingers by the door talking to Eber, who always indulges him, no matter how long-winded he gets. Eber's getting paid by the hour, so maybe listening to Bill's raving beats looking out at the deserted street. He tries to talk Bill out of riding his bike home. Offers to pay for a car. Bill insists he's fine.

Next morning I see him at the coffee shop. A jagged stream of dried blood snakes from the left side of his forehead down his cheek, coming to a stop three-quarters of the way down his shirt. He says he took a spill riding home but has no memory of how, nor of standing lost with his pants down in the bathroom at the bar. He apologizes if he caused any trouble. Says I should always tell him if he's out of line. Then asks what music I'm listening to on my iPod.

It's an old trap. I say goodbye and walk away.

Dirtbag Dick

Dick was a doorman at the Albatross when Lon hired me. A scraggly stick-figure of a guy. He's a junkie drunk out of central casting. Why anyone would entrust a wastoid like him with the most menial job is beyond me.

Lon tried him out behind the bar once, only to come back and find the bar unlocked, glasses strewn everywhere, Dick passed out asleep on the corner stool. He busted him back down to doorman rather than showing him the door. Lon has a soft heart. He won't throw anything or anyone away if he can help it.

Once I came on, Dick would send me five- and ten-screen texts detailing the reasons why he needed me to cover his shift. Why do guys like him always assume everyone wants to know their life story? Just ask and I'll say yes or no. No explanation necessary.

Eventually he stopped showing up, and I took over his shifts for good. Word was he'd gotten a job at a micro-brewery down the street. They're popping up like mushrooms these days. I imagine him meeting his maker toppling into a vat of sour.

Whenever he comes back to the Albatross now, he's plastered. As often as not, I don't serve him a single drink. Just tell whoever he showed up with to take him out of here. It helps that he has no memory of who I am. He introduces himself and wants to shake hands every single time.

Like a cockroach the guy just won't die. I see him late night outside the Ceevus looking like the coverboy for *Meth Monthly*. He's a walking *Scared Straight* after-school special. And yet, he has friends. Women who want to be with him. What's his secret? Do they hate themselves so much they need to be attached to someone like Dick to make sure everybody knows? He's like a mascot for giving up.

One day he comes into the Albatross and he's sober as a judge. He greets me by name and orders a beer. Then a shot and another beer. Then another shot. His eyes glaze over and he has trouble navigating to the men's room. The switch has been thrown. He's reverted back to the way I'm used to him being.

Dirtbag Dick: one of the wonders of the neighborhood.

Impostor

Jay shows up during the rare rushes after 2 am. He cozies up to this or that cluster of drinkers. Most know him and accept him, though everyone keeps him at a distance. He buys a round of shots and laughs louder than the rest at their tired quips. Most have known one another for decades, their banter well-worn and instinctive as breath, while Jay's attempts always ring false.

Too young, too clean, too smooth, too quick to try to engage. Whatever his angle is, he misses by a mile. Amid the sad lushes, angry hicks, and disgruntled cops who haunt the Blue Light, he's all wrong.

Why does he come here? The Blue Light is not a place to make friends or find love. It's a closed society. Everyone here plays their role: the everyday joe who needs two shots and a beer to get a kind word out; the over-the-hill party girl desperate for just one more night as belle of the ball; the old man who's seen it all and told it all the same way over and over and over again; the ugly couple who take their bedroom fights out to the bar to make themselves sound more interesting than they actually are; the angry alcoholic looking to focus his anger at a fixed target. Jay is none of these.

His phony chumminess rubs me the wrong way, but we tolerate one another until the night I cut him off. He gets louder and louder until I have no choice but to kick him out. Now he's no longer so friendly. Seething, threatening, dark eyes flashing fury, he refuses to leave. Because I have no doorman nor coworkers for back-up, I have to just pretend he's not there. He hangs around another half hour casting his death stare my way, then walks out, promising he'll be back.

At closing time, he's lurking in the shadows across from the door, peering out from between the columns of the underpass. Forty-five minutes later, with the glasses clean, empties tossed, chairs up, and bar gleaming wet, I look out the front window and don't see him. I walk to the bus stop like always, wondering when I'll see him again.

A Pool Table is Bad News

Matt and Laura come to the Blue Light every week. They order a pitcher of Old Style and play pool. The table is at the back of the bar, and players have to stand aside to let guys get to the men's room on one side, women to the ladies' on the other. Every game is interrupted multiple times. There's no way around it.

Matt and Laura claim they're not together, but their games look more like dates the less beer's left in the pitcher. She brushes against him before lining up the next shot. She keeps looking at him while he's lining up his. She kisses the back of his neck. He laughs it off.

If they order a second pitcher, she gets weepy before it's half gone. He pushes her away when she whispers in his ear. Some nights after they've been in, I go home and dream about her. It's a generic man's dream. I push Matt aside and Laura wants me instead. But the pool table punctures the fantasy. Nothing started around a barroom pool table ever ends well.

It's a quiet afternoon but I'm uneasy. Geoff is in with a coworker from his garage. They rack up a game. They're on their lunch break pounding bottles of Icehouse and Rumple Minze. Loser pays. Geoff goes to the jukebox and feeds it a dollar to play Kid Rock's "Cowboy" five times in a row.

I try to tune it out, but soon they're screaming at each other. Geoff is accusing his pal of cheating. Now they're fencing with their pool cues. I go back there and ask what the problem is. Geoff apologizes as I take the sticks out of their hands. They go up to the bar and order another round before returning to work.

The worst is when a guy hogs the table. After he wins a couple games, he becomes insufferable. Then, as others get impatient for their chance, people get testy. Jimmy picks up the quarter that marked his place in line, but Tim insists it was his. Everyone else joins in, takes sides. They nearly come to blows. I shut down the table for the night.

At the Albatross, there's no pool table. There's a dartboard but we lost or broke most of the darts long ago and tell people it's out of order. Sometimes old-timers come in and insist there used to be a table. But Lon tells them there hasn't been one in fifty years. He's spent his whole life here so he'd know. They walk away muttering to themselves, not convinced.

What is it about a felt-covered table with holes that inspires so much misery? Nothing good ever happens around one. It's a magnet for misfortune. Maybe it's the booze that turns the game bad, but I've never been anywhere that drinks weren't a part of it. The more players drink, the more the balls and cues become weapons.

I flinch hearing the hard clap of balls hitting each other. It's only a matter of time before one ends up on the floor or airborne, aimed at somebody's head. Then I have to go back and end the game, and they hate me for it. Maybe they can't enjoy themselves without a threat of danger. There are no stakes otherwise.

When Matt and Laura leave, they're not speaking to each other. Whatever she's trying to get him to do falls on deaf ears. Maybe the pool table's not to blame, but it doesn't help.

Jukeboxes are also no good. Drinkers can be trusted with neither.

The Professor Smells

I think he's pissed himself again. Lon has taken him aside a bunch of times to ask that he doesn't come in with soiled drawers. Good thing his time is afternoons when the bar is mostly deserted. Still, who wants to have to hold his breath at work?

The worst part is that he never acknowledges it. Never apologizes. Never leaves without being told to. I just have to pretend it doesn't smell. Pete motions me over to the window and whispers about it, as if there's any way I could miss it.

Pete and the Professor are thick as thieves but bitch about each other to me any chance they get. They're in every day.

The problem is that they're like the same side of a magnet; two self-professed sages. The Professor will drone on for hours about whatever item in the Times catches his eye and Pete knows more about you than you do. He'll insult you if you disagree. I learned my lesson early and agree with everything he says. It drives him crazy. The Professor is a little harder to read. It's never clear whether he cares if I'm listening or not, just needs a direction at which to lecture.

But right now all I know is he's pissed himself again. I have to call Lon to get him out of here. Lon has said not to embarrass him so I don't, but Lon is gone on one of his errands and doesn't answer his cell. How long can I keep holding my breath. The old guy sits there oblivious, slowly turning the pages of his newspaper, taking a pull off his Old Style now and then.

Pete pokes his nose against the diamond window in the front door to check who's in the bar before pushing it open and walking in. He does this every time. Every day. I wonder who it would take to be sitting here for Pete to turn around and leave?

Nobody knows where he's coming from or where he goes after drinking his fill of Old Style at the Albatross. His clothes aren't weathered enough for him to be homeless, but it's hard to imagine him having a home. He carries a knapsack and several bags on him at all times. His nose is always running.

I bring his beer without prompting, not that he bothers to ask. He was here long before me and thinks he'll be here long after I'm gone. He's probably right. I don't have to say a thing for him to know I hate him. Many days Pete and the Professor sit together, giving me a corner of the bar to avoid.

Every five beers, Pete grudgingly leaves an extra crumpled dollar. He always makes sure I notice. Half his stays at the bar are taken up rolling Top tobacco into cigarettes, leaving the dregs all around where he sits. He makes a show of packing up his belongings, side-eying the other drinkers, before ducking out for a smoke. The routine is repeated dozens of times a night. Pete makes me grateful for the smoking ban because it means a few minutes every hour I'm free of him.

The worst times are when he has a woman with him. How much does she have to hate herself to be with this cockroach? I hope he pays them well. I know he pays for the drinks. Then everyone has to watch him gum her with his toothless maw. It's like those medieval Dance of Death scenes. I wish the image would fade, but it will be with me to my dying breath.

Pete's a snoop and a know-it-all. He eavesdrops and inserts himself into others' conversations. One time when "Walk on the Wild Side" came on he announced to everyone within earshot that it was Lou Reed's only hit. No one asked.

What I like best is that he leaves without saying goodbye. I know that's a French Exit, but what do you call it when somebody no one wants to see never returns? What country is that named after? Russia? Timbuktu? How can I make it so Pete never comes back?

World Champion
of Poland

His friend, the Captain, hypes him like a professional pro-
motor. Do I know who this man is? He's the former world
boxing champion of Poland! Do they expect me to bow or
let him drink on the house? Sharon says to make every fifth
drink free but nothing about comping dignitaries. The man
himself is humble and soft-spoken. He's in his fifties maybe
but retains a fighter's physique. In a wife-beater his faded tat-

toos are visible on each shoulder. They look amateur, maybe from the army.

He barely drinks what the Captain puts in front of him, just stares off into the distance. He looks like he's mourning something long-gone that he can't remember. I have nothing to say to him so I don't. He doesn't mind the silence. He's not desperate to fill it like his pal. The Captain can't shut up. Everything about him is loud including his Hawaiian shirt. I don't know what he's captain of except he wears the cap. I bet he'd go overboard his first voyage.

One evening at the Albatross, I see an obit in the *Trib*. I recognize the broken pug's nose and far-away eyes. He really was a boxing champion but not of Poland. He never left Chicago aside from his time in the service. He won the Gold Gloves then turned pro for a time. He trained kids. He had some hand in political circles. Johnny Something. I never knew his name at the bar because the Captain kept yelling about all he'd done without bothering to introduce us. I never knew the Captain's name either. I wouldn't recognize him in an obit without his cap and Hawaiian shirt. I learned nothing true about the man.

So many of the regulars were just nicknames. Hillbilly, the Captain, Timmie the Cabbie, Chopper, Rocky. It's the way they wanted to be known. At first they wanted to give me one too, but I flat refused. It was their way of welcoming me, but I didn't want to be welcomed. I held myself apart.

It's different at the Albatross. I have history here. I feel like I belong. For every time I confuse the two bars, this is the thing that sets them apart. No matter what problem I have with Bill or the Professor or anyone else, I feel like they're of my world and I'm of theirs. At the Blue Light, I never felt that way.

When I first wrote about the Blue Light, I subtitled it *My Year Sitting Ringside to Hell*. I thought I was a visitor in a foreign place, an observer reporting on somebody else's world. If the Albatross is also a hell, then I am one of its devils. I can't hold myself at arm's length here.

Dead Rae

Inez comes into the Albatross to ask about Rae. Inez lives in Texas and knows Rae's brother. He showed her some of Rae's art and Inez is hooked. Now she wants to write something about it. Make Rae famous. That's why she's here. It's causing me to think about someone I don't like to think about.

When her brother wrote me about her death seven years ago, I'd been out of touch with Rae a long time. I had to cut her out of my life. She caused a lot of damage. Or, more accurately, my knowing her had. My connection to her had contributed to the end of her marriage, the cancellation of mine, dozens of failed friendships, and more hurt feelings, confusion, and drama than I can account for. Now a bright-eyed new person has appeared to dredge up what I thought was dead and buried. And yet, I try to answer all the questions Inez asks. In answering, I realize how little I know about a woman I thought I knew too well.

I met Rae through her then-boyfriend/ex-husband-to-be at Hoax Cafe. They'd recently moved to Chicago from California, and he was concerned that she didn't have any friends in their new town. He knew I made art, so Rae and I would have something to talk about. She waited tables at Leo's Lunchroom down the street, but apart from bumming cigarettes off me, she rarely said a word. Soon after Cal introduced us, she was making covert dinner plans with me. I didn't understand why the fact we were going for pasta at Club Lucky had to be kept a secret, but soon learned that if Rae wasn't scheming or setting people in her life against each other, she didn't feel alive. I played along because I realized it was the price of admission. It was fascinating watching her gears turn. She never stopped spinning fantasies.

She told coworkers at Leo's she had cancer when she didn't, told me and others her oldest brother was dead when he wasn't. Even when caught in a bald-faced lie, she rarely acknowledged it. She'd massage and massage her explanations until we either gave up or forgot about it. Everyone knew she couldn't live without her lies. I took any childhood story she told as a fairy tale, so it was a surprise when I eventually met her parents and one of her brothers; I'd just assumed she'd made them all up. Some of the things she said about them were even true.

Rae and Cal broke up for a time, and she moved in with me. She immediately took up with one of Cal's coworkers at the coffee shop. Kurt was a blackout drunk. I remember carrying him up the stairs with my next-door neighbor Liam after Kurt had passed out on Liam's porch, mistaking it for ours. I had to throw out a loveseat because Kurt soaked it with his urine, and Rae had to get rubber sheets for her bed because he pissed himself nightly. Then Rae reconciled with Cal and they got married. I wasn't invited to the wedding.

We kept in touch though. I watched her invent and reinvent herself. She knew she could count on me, which meant that I got tangled up in her dramas. Shiv and I made plans to marry during this time. Shiv used my relationship with Rae as one of her reasons for leaving me. Cal hated me. The day I drove a car full of Shiv's belongings down south where she'd moved after breaking up with me, Cal chased the car down the street threatening to beat me up. I just laughed and kept driving. When I crossed the Texas border, it was raining sideways, so hard the wipers couldn't keep up and the skies were black. Every rest stop was full of stopped vehicles. I found out the next day I was within a few miles of a tornado.

Back in Chicago, Rae started cooking for the Archdiocese of Chicago, and we resumed our weird relationship. Through the church, she met an old rich man who became fixated on her. He moved her into his downtown condo. But she was never happy with just one man's attention. She posed for me one afternoon, and on a break from working, we started messing around. If her roommate hadn't walked in, who knows what might've been, but afterwords she got shy and said it had been a mistake. We never finished the painting, but another old man/admirer bought it as is for $500 in order to curry favor with her. I was happy to be rid of it and to take his money.

Rae always drank like a fish. Red wine was her poison, and she'd drink bottles, rarely eating much aside from dry toast or popcorn. I'd insist we go out for dinner because that was the only way she'd eat properly. Eventually, her doctors told her she was on the brink of liver failure. She stopped working, letting the old men take care of her. Then she moved back to California. But by then I'd stopped answering her phone calls. Friends called her an emotional vampire, and maybe that's what she was.

I'd reclaimed a lot of her favorite tunes as my own in the years after my involvement with Rae ended. I could listen to Cat Power, Smog, and Silver Jews, and not immediately remember her playing them on repeat behind her closed bedroom door. Since Inez got in touch, when I put one of them on, Rae's in the room with me again. I tell Inez that I don't care much for Rae's art. It was always a sore point for her. She knew I didn't like her dramatic birds beneath cracking varnish or her tormented self-portraits. I found them as phony as most of her stories.

But Inez is convinced Rae's art is worth celebrating. Inez tells me Rae's brother is no longer cooperating with her.

Seems his new fiancée is uncomfortable with their friendship. So Rae's legacy of ruining relationships survives her. I doubt Inez will come up with enough for a substantive biographical document. Most of the people who knew Rae around here are long gone, the places she worked are changed or no longer exist. I dig up some correspondence and postcards I'd saved and give them to Inez for her research. It's good to be rid of them.

Maybe Inez can write a fairy tale about a scary-thin girl with long blond hair who liked to tell tall tales. That would be a fitting tribute.

Hazel

Hazel texts and Lon looks worried. Sometimes he says he lives with her; other times he has to run out because she tells him she's just put something of his out in the alley. He gets panicked because to Lon every single thing he owns is a treasure. He can let nothing go.

Hazel's family runs the last of the old stockyard slaughterhouses. Come the holidays, she lays out quite the spread at the bar. Steaming trays of kielbasa, corned beef and cabbage, meat lasagna, pierogis. The moochers go apeshit. They never eat so well the rest of the year.

Hazel is scary. I know Lon is afraid the way he cowers when she's around. I don't always know what she's mad about, but it's her resting state. Fortunately for the rest of us, her ire is mostly pointed Lon's way. We're all quietly grateful not to be involved with her as we watch her chew him out.

One day Lon announces they're through. Seems she's been stepping out on Lon with one of his oldest friends. He can take the belittlement and abuse, but this is a betrayal beyond the pale. The trips to pick up his belongings in the alley become a daily thing.

Lon closes the bar sometimes and asks me to come when it's something big like a sideboard or an antique mirror. The antique mechanical bingo machine is the most precarious. We manage not to wreck it between the alley and the bar, but as soon as we set it down on the counter, the glass enclosure holding the numbered balls shatters as if shot by a sniper. We spend hours cleaning up the slivers and shards. The bar doesn't open till nearly 7 p.m. that day.

After they break up, Lon calls her every last name in the book but refuses to throw away the Kasperski Meats calendar behind the bar. The one proudly advertising pork boners and butts. He did Sharpie out *Kasperski*. Lon just can't bear to throw anything away. Even when it rubs his nose in humiliation and bad feeling.

Football

The first couple hours are painfully slow. A few of the regulars—the ones who come every afternoon—show, but otherwise it's crickets till 8:30 p.m. I'm so bored I text Eber at ten past the hour, thinking he's late; he isn't supposed to be in till 9 p.m. Then a bunch of people I've never seen in the bar before pile in. Most are pretty far along already, doubtless turned out of some place that has wall-to-wall flatscreens. They want bombs, shots, and want to start tabs on their credit cards.

A lot of pent up testosterone and frustration in the room. After hours of idling, they have me running around. It's hard to switch gears so fast. I don't mind when the bar is busy, I can handle it, but the night has a bad vibe, an angry edge to it. Maybe they're all mad Tom Brady won another ring or are just mean drunks. In any case, serving them brings me no joy.

A guy comes up irate that the pint of Old Style he forgot at his table fifteen minutes before taking a single sip doesn't taste fresh. I offer to replace it but he acts put out, as if I'm disrespecting him, tells me he's been coming here ten years, that I can't do him like that. I tell him to leave. Eber has to escort him and his embarrassed, apologizing friends out the door.

I miss it, but Elvin's best friend starts choking him out at one of the tables, so Eber has to bum-rush him as well. There are often months when I don't have to eighty-six a single drinker.

A couple on an internet date keep trying to monopolize my attention, making me part of their conversation. She asks me whether, as a newly-single woman, she has the right to tell dates that she is up for flirting, but not down to fuck. He gets mock-angry that I take her side. Then she insists on touching my beard, making her date unhappy for real.

Later a very young, very drunk and disoriented man keeps asking to use the bar's telephone. He doesn't know the number he's trying to dial or even how he's gotten to the Albatross. We repeatedly give him directions to Celine's, where he says his brother is, but he keeps coming back in and trying to use the phone. The last time he comes in he comes up to the bar and orders two Modelos. We don't serve Modelo. Eber makes him give him cash and pushes him into an Uber. After closing time, we go out to the back lot and find the kid's car, one of the headlights smashed in, all four tires flat. It's a miracle he didn't kill anybody.

I hate football.

Casanova at
the Corner Bar

I pay the guy no mind the first couple times he comes up. Young, kind of conceited-sounding, typical. He sits toward the back of the bar with a couple acting like they are on a date. But as the night wears on, he becomes a problem. He begins to linger at the bar, chatting up whoever is nearest. He acts in a way that forces us to watch him. But he isn't the only distraction this night.

Riley always has stories about people who come in. She knows everyone. Who's with who; who they used to be with; which one is stepping out on their significant other; which ones are trying out an open arrangement. I like hearing her stories. Tonight I have one for her for a change.

Brandy comes in with her boyfriend and takes a booth as usual. She doesn't acknowledge my presence. That's been her way the last few years, but it wasn't always.

When I moved back to the neighborhood, Brandy and I had a fling. She was a grad student and interviewed me for a class. That's how it started. She was half my age—it was as clichéd as all get out. The troubles began when I told Shiv about it. It never crossed my mind it would be a problem.

It was a big problem. Shiv took my being with Brandy as a personal affront, like I was doing it to hurt her. The truth was much worse: I didn't think of her at all when I went home with Brandy.

I broke it off after a month because Brandy wanted a boyfriend and I wasn't boyfriend material. It was just nice to be wanted for a change. She didn't take the breakup well. She started taking Tinder dates to the bar on nights I worked and making a show of making out with them. It was a different guy every time. I was amused and wondered how much of it was for my benefit. If any of it was, she didn't know me very well. We live in the same neighborhood, so we'd run into each other occasionally. It was usually cordial but awkward. Then, a year or two ago, she started showing up with the same guy—a dorky mustachioed fellow, much younger than the ones she used to go with. He looked to be her age. I was happy she found someone.

I tell Riley all this as we watch Brandy's boyfriend tuck his napkin like a bib into his shirt collar like a senior citizen before wolfing down an Italian beef. Meanwhile, our problem customer is firing questions at a woman sitting by herself and obviously not looking for company. She politely answers him when he asks what she does for a living (cosmetics rep) and even asks what he does (used to sell suits, now works some office job.) But she barely makes eye contact, doesn't swivel her barstool his way, and keeps scrolling her cellphone. He talks and talks, forgetting the round of drinks he ordered and was supposed to bring back to his table. The couple back there is practically making babies now, so I don't entirely blame him for staying away.

He wobbles his way to the bathroom, and the girl he'd been talking to immediately bolts out the door. Then he's back with his friends, with his shirt off. I ask Eber to tell him to put it back on. Apparently he is showing off a new tattoo. Eber reminds him our bar is not clothing-optional.

Next time he comes up for a round, he's having some trouble focusing. I pour the two beers, then instantly regret it. He takes a sip, then spends fifteen minutes close-talking a guy at the bar with the same persistence he did with the girl. His target humors him the best he can, though he's obviously uncomfortable. Then Casanova wanders away, forgetting his beers. I empty them in the sink.

He's back half an hour later to order more, but I tell him he's had enough. He's confused but stumbles away without a fight. He sits back down and watches his friends make out. Then returns to ask for beer again, forgetting he's been cut off. It's last call now and I make the first of three trips back to where he's sitting to ask him and his friends to go home. On one of my visits, after I thank them for coming in, he shoots back, —Thanks for what? I hesitate a second but walk away. When they finally leave, the whole area where they'd been is covered in shredded coasters, M & M's lodged in the seat cushions, as if they were squirrels or birds scattering materials around a nest.

On my walk home after closing the bar, I see him sitting on the sidewalk by an underpass. His phone is by his side, lit up, blaring dance music. His head lolls back and forth. I almost stop to see if he's okay, but keep walking.

Aggressive or Insane?

Monday night.

A guy in his late twenties sits right where the sinks are. He orders an Old Style and thanks me profusely, then goes back to casting his serial-killer eyes around the room. He comes to the bar pretty regularly but usually takes a table in the back. Where he sits tonight there's no way I can ignore him.

He tries to make small talk, but it comes off as veiled insults. He's going for jocular humor maybe, but the results are the non sequitur logic of a lunatic. I can't tell how aware he is of what he sounds like. I look back down at the pint glasses

I'm rinsing, then wander down the bar, acting as if I have something to do, aside from getting away from him.

He orders a Schlitz tallboy, then summons me back a few minutes later and sticks out his thumb for me to look at. He claims there was a piece of glass on the lip of the can, but I see nothing. I pass my fingers over the remaining cans in the cooler just to make sure, then offer him one on the house for his trouble.

A couple beers later he's muttering to himself and attempting conversations with neighboring drinkers, who pretend not to hear him. He asks politely for one last beer, and, after hesitating a moment, I comply. Fifteen minutes later, he asks for another. I tell him I think he had the right idea last time. He wants to know why. I explain that in my professional opinion he's had enough, that he's talking to himself, and harassing other patrons.

—So it's because I'm being aggressive, not crazy, right?

I let it hang there, then start to walk away. He mumbles something about he'll remember how he was treated here and stalks out.

Can't wait till next time. There's always a next time with guys like him.

Friend of the Owner

I see Eber going over to one of the booths. He's talking to Jeff, a neighborhood guy who's always creeped me out. I motion Eber over and ask what's going on. A young woman in the next booth has complained that Jeff is harassing her.

A little later I see the woman walk up to the door where Eber's posted. Jeff's eyes are glued on her the whole way. Eber's shoulders slump. Then he walks back to Jeff's booth and asks him to leave. Jeff wants to know why. Says he's done nothing wrong. Refuses to get up. Eber goes back to his post. I see him talking on his phone.

Three minutes later two Chicago Police officers come in. They exchange a word with Eber, then go over to Jeff's booth and loom over him the way cops do.

The Albatross isn't the Blue Light. There's no police station across the street, and Lon has never encouraged the men and women in blue to think of his bar as their own. There are a couple cops who are regulars, but they never come in in uniform and would never think of putting their service weapon on the bar next to their pints. It's not that kind of place.

In my years here, I've never called the cops on anyone.

They're to be avoided unless you want to make a bad situation worse. So it's a shock to see these two in here. I wish Eber had asked me before calling them. He's not a tough guy and isn't in the habit of putting his hands on people. He must've felt like he had no other choice. Everyone else in the place is now looking at Jeff's booth; conversation has stopped, dates have been interrupted, because cops are here and something is about to go down.

I walk over and Jeff looks my way, expecting to be rescued. He insists he's done nothing wrong. He keeps repeating it. Says he didn't even talk to the woman. Her friends tell a different story. She stays silent. Seeing that he's not getting anywhere, Jeff insists I call Lon. I ask him what that would accomplish. I tell him that Lon would tell him to leave just like we are. If he was Lon's friend, he would have respect for his bar.

The cops, inpatient for action, start moving closer to Jeff to escort him out. That makes him get up. He loudly protests his innocence all the way out the door. A pall hangs over the bar for an hour after they've gone. Something of the sanctity of our place has been violated and needs time to be restored. I send over a round of shots to the woman's booth to smooth the transition.

Near closing time, Jeff appears at the door trying to apologize. I tell him to come back another day.

I see him and his wife at the pool in the park down the street a few months later. I take care not to meet his eye. But daylight is good cover for a bartender. In sunshine, half-naked, we look nothing like we do in darkness among the taps and bottles.

NO MORE JAZZ MONDAYS

Korb rearranges the chairs at 4pm every Monday. He makes them all face the little makeshift stage in the back of the Albatross. It's hours until anyone will show up to listen to his free jazz combo try the regulars' patience by alternating squalls of piercing atonal brass notes with barely audible string noodling. But Korb measures the gaps between seats as if he's at the Village Vanguard before Coltrane hits the stage.

I give the guy credit. His monastic devotion to a narrow definition of pure musical expression is sort of admirable, if a bit creepy. He's a little white suburban kid who worships at an altar built of the frustration and struggle of the descendants of former slaves. What can Korb possibly contribute that doesn't smack of imitation or outright thievery? Yet, it's mostly guys like Korb, fanatical followers with little primal connection, who keep this stuff alive.

Mondays are slow at the bar, so when Korb asks Lon about hosting a music night it seems pretty low risk. The place is empty anyway. Why not let the kid invite his friends to play their weird music? Few of them drink much. They duck their heads into their coats to vape in between sips of dollar Old Style. But maybe if there are more of them it could be worthwhile.

The first night, Korb's band clears the room in ten minutes. Even Bill, who will linger if there's anyone at all in the bar to talk at, sprints out the door. I lean my elbows on the bar and give in to the pain the three guys onstage are inflicting on their instruments. The three nearest chairs are occupied by their significant others. Tough to say whether they're enjoying the sounds their mates produce. Pleasure isn't the point. This is art. It's supposed to be difficult, incomprehensible, unpleasant.

Korb hunches over his saxophone directing all the force he can summon through it, producing a tone which makes me imagine a particularly painful alien birth. His drummer scrapes and stabs at his kit with objects salvaged from the alley out back. The bassist mostly air guitars his upright's strings while freeze-framing in various dramatic poses.

Afterwards, Korb passes his Kangol cap around for donations. Lon has given him an open tab for the night plus $50, so this feels wrong. Besides, does he expect his girlfriend to pay for listening? Should probably be the other way around. But guys like him never know that. He believes his audience, whoever it's made up of, is given great privilege by witnessing him do his thing. He's doing important work.

He sure as hell won't get a dime out of me.

Since no one is ordering drinks, I sketch them playing. After a few weeks of Mondays I fill up half a book. There are now about a dozen faithful listeners and Korb's combo isn't the only one that performs. Carey shows up once, but doesn't sit in, though Korb begs him to. The regulars know to clear out at 7pm sharp.

Things come to a head the night Korb loses it on a birthday party.

Three middle-aged women and their husbands are crowded in the booth furthest from the stage. They come in right after I open. They've brought a birthday cake, candles, paper plates. They order shots of Jaëger before sitting down. They put candles in the cake, light them, and sing happy birthday. The birthday girl, dressed in a blouse for her 20-year-old self, blows them out with such force that she almost lands on the floor from the recoil.

They cut up the cake and bring me and the drinkers at the bar slices. Then a round of Old Style and more Jaëger. They're getting a little loud but not bothering anybody, so I let them be.

Korb walks in carrying his horn. He nods my way, puts his things down near the stage and starts to move chairs. He gives the party a dirty look now and then. It's not even 5pm. The band starts at 7.

All the chairs now point toward the stage. Each table and place at the bar has a flier with Korb's music schedule for the next three months. He lights tea candles and distributes them about the room. He skips the party, but they don't notice. They're scream-laughing as he passes them.

As 7pm approaches all the regulars clear out. A dozen young people in carefully chosen thrift-store garb cluster near the stage in the back. A few are talking to Korb and his bandmates. Some scribble intently in tiny notebooks, the rest stare into space. None are drinking.

The birthday party near the door is still raging even though I've cut them off. The last three times any of them come up to order Jaëger I offer pint glasses of water instead. They'll leave eventually. But not soon enough for Korb.

After setting up the instruments and passing the Kangol around the crowd preemptively, he marches over to the party and tells them to be quiet. He's not yelling but his tone isn't friendly. They stop for a second, look up at him in unison, then burst into laughter. Korb skulks back to the stage and proceeds to lead his combo in a paint-peeling half hour of improvised noise. The birthday party departs at about the mid-way point, as they're unable to hear one another even when they scream. I fill up a couple sketchbook pages, then go pick up the dozen empty shot glasses, piles of paper plates, and crumpled napkins and wrapping paper.

Lon comes down just as Korb is packing up his sax. He gives him the customary $50, but says this is the last time. He tells me later somebody from the party, a former schoolmate, it turns out, called and complained. After everyone else is gone, Korb sits slumped over his Old Style and complains that he's been mistreated. That nobody understands his art. I pause a moment or two for sympathy, then go back to washing glasses.

Korb comes in sometimes but he leaves the chairs where they are. The regulars have started to stay past 7pm again.

When someone asks about live music at the Albatross I tell them about Korb.

Black Emerald

I'm at the Albatross with my coffee and breakfast sandwich to babysit the bar as it's being prepped for a film shoot. I'd bartended the night before and seen the newly-green walls and faux-Irish bar decor. I'd listened to the grumbling of the regulars and watched the dumbfounded glances of patrons trying to put a finger on what was different at the bar this night. Others came in like any other night. They were there to drink and what was or wasn't up on the walls was of no concern to them whatsoever.

Lon instructs me to watch that they don't tear the place apart, then takes off. I open my laptop to try to do some work but keep looking around as the crew works away to ready the room for shooting the following day. They have to do as much as they can while still leaving the bar operational for that evening's regular non-movie business. The booze, beer tap, glassware, and bar itself remain as they've always been; everything else is off.

The barstools are now wooden and have backs, rather than round and vinyl with chrome legs. There are many, many more tables, and each one has its own little lamp with its own little lampshade. The Oddfellows banners are replaced by Boston T signs for a fictional Orange Line stop called Dover. There are now photos of various Kennedys and not a single one of Anton Cermak. A neon above the back door promises live music but doesn't elaborate. A sign over the ladies' room says *Sláinte* in Irish bar Gaelic font. The CSI pinball machine is replaced by a Wurlitzer jukebox.

I watch a lighting tech test out light strips placed behind the bottles of liquor. She manipulates virtual dials on her tablet to make them change into a succession of hideously bright colors. There are also strips of green light to illuminate the front of the bar down to the floor. She tells me about the other shows she's worked on, which include the whole variety-pack of Dick Wolf franchises. She doesn't think any more of those than I do, but we both agree that it's good that locals get jobs on these shows even if they have nothing to do with Chicago and little with basic human decency.

The show they'll be shooting here the next day will have nothing to do with Chicago either. The Albatross is to play a South Boston bar called the Black Emerald in a pilot for a TV show based on Ben Affleck's *Gone Baby Gone*. I ask Lon before he leaves whether they'll paint the walls brown again and he says no, because if the series gets picked up and they want to shoot here again, they'd just have to repaint it all over again.

As an electrician opens one of the curio cabinets in the back bar, he turns to me and asks if the tchotchkes and keepsakes are theirs or ours. —Ours, so please leave them as they are, I say, and feel like I've done my job for the day.

The day after the shoot, I come in to see if the Albatross is the Albatross again. Aside from the green walls, everything else is mostly back in place. I ask Rose what she thinks of the walls, and she says it wouldn't have been her choice but that it looks clean.

Who would argue against a free paint job?

Pink Eye

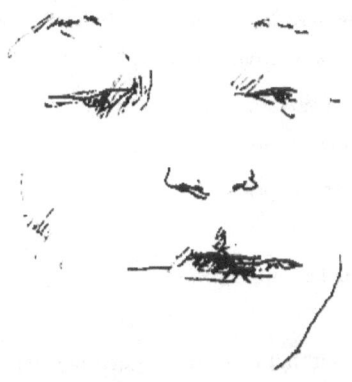

Eber walks a guy over from the door. Tells me he needs directions. The guy moves slow. It takes him forever to unfold a packet of papers, then find the place on the sheet with the address he's looking for. It's the Pacific Garden Mission—the homeless shelter a mile away.

—I've been walking all day, he says. Then asks for a glass of water and some napkins.

His face is swollen around the eyes and his features are off, like they're the wrong proportions. Every movement takes forever. He dabs at one of his eyes, leaving stains on the tissue after each touch. He says he's happy the shelter's close—he thought he was still many miles off. Then he asks for a drink on the house. When I say no, he asks how much it would be if it wasn't on the house. I tell him I wouldn't be comfortable serving him a drink at any price.

—You think I'm fucked up, right?

I say I don't know but that he won't be getting a drink here.

—Can you make sense of this? he asks, fanning out his packet of papers. It's from Stroger Hospital. Intake information, diagnoses, and directions for aftercare. I say I don't know.

—This is what they say I got. Pink Eye. You know how you get it? It's from shit. Wipe your ass, then rub your eyes. The doc said I should get better by the twentieth, that's when I turn twenty-two. But I don't know.

Then he asks if I heard about Banksy's latest stupid art world stunt. Even skid row bums know about that clown.

I walk away to pretend to serve my three remaining customers, but mostly for a break from the man's misery. When I go back to him, he tells me I should probably throw away the glass I served him water in. That it might be contagious.

—If it's not one thing it's another. Let me give you a piece of advice: Don't ever mess up.

I thank him for the wisdom and reiterate the directions to Pacific Garden Mission.

He takes several more minutes to gather his papers and stuff them slow-motion into his pocket, then points his body towards the door.

After he clears the threshold, I throw the glass he used in the trash.

Christmas at the Bar

Everyone else wants Christmas off, so I volunteer to come in and keep the bar open. Lon is surprised. He never remembers I don't celebrate. We agree on opening at 8 p.m. rather than the normal 4.

I catch a movie in the afternoon, then get some Chinese food; even though the High Holidays mean as little to me as Jesus' birthday, I am still a Jew.

It's dark inside. Lon's mom is away, spending Christmas with her other son. Lon is there too. It's eerie to be here when no one else is. Captain Beefheart keeps me company as I put down chairs, turn on lights, fill up the ice wells, and cut fruit.

I flip the neon and unlock the front door just as Eber is walking up. He's also an unbeliever. Though he has to go through the motions with his wife's family in the burbs.

No one comes in the first hour, but then they start to trickle in. Some familiar faces, some strangers; all happy the bar is open. On holidays the Albatross is a refuge. A place to go after fulfilling familial responsibilities. A spot to exhale. I wonder why they go through the trouble because it makes them so miserable. Why go into debt buying presents nobody needs, why pretend to get along with relatives you hate, why I act this one day in a way you never would the other 364 days of the year?

What really runs the ring up is endless shots. Five, seven, ten pours of Malört, rail whiskey, Cazadores, Fernet, Stoli, Fireball, SoCo for those pretending they're still in high school. I run out of clean shot glasses and dip into the rocks tumblers. Every free surface is covered in dirty glassware. I wash one stack only to see Eber bringing three more. It's this way all night. But I'm not complaining.

I don't turn up my nose at holiday tips. Drinkers show their appreciation in a quantifiable way on this day to a degree they don't on any other. If Jesus is responsible for that, then I praise him. I make about half a month's rent this night.

Disappearing Girl

Anna's not a regular but I've seen her in here before. I have a thing for her. I bring her a beer and we chat a minute, but then some guy shows and joins her so I walk away.

They talk about tattoos. Both are pretty well covered. She tells him she cheated on her long-term boyfriend, who's been away working in Alaska, with a guy she with whom she has nothing in common. Their love ends when her pitbull bites half his middle finger off. She puts it on ice like you're supposed to, but they can't reattach it. The dog has to be put down. Despite this they keep seeing each other. Then his family convinces him to sue her. She breaks it off with him. Starts seeing someone new. This one still has all ten digits for the moment.

Anna isn't through her first beer when the pitbull victim comes through the door with a friend. I'd never seen him at the bar with anyone but her and since the lawsuit he hasn't been coming around.

They're not sitting near each other. Anna usually stays for a few rounds, but I see her gathering her things as if to leave.

When I walk by the two men, the friend is off on a rant.

—I'm giving up on love. I realize I'm only twenty-seven, but my best years are behind me. I was real popular in high-school. Fucked a different girl like every week?

—A woman? She needs to learn to suck cock, to cook, and not complain about doing the dishes if she wants to be a housewife…Bitches cause all the bad shit but they got pussies and I'm addicted to that shit.

Anna disappears. I think she's gone to the bathroom. I knock on the door and whisper her name, hoping to wake her without disturbing the other drinkers. I don't want them seeing what's happening if she's passed out. No response. I go back to pouring beer. Half an hour later, I ask Eber to check the door and he opens it. No one's inside.

Viral

Sunday night before the lockdown is a busy one at the bar. I'm surprised, figuring people would prefer to stay away and not tempt fate. Instead, it's an end-of-the-world-party vibe. Everyone recognizes it will be some time till we can meet this way again and we make the most of it.

John comes in with a woman I don't know. He's a bartender and musician. He always seems resigned and apathetic, but not this night. He's positively giddy. I see the guy smile more times within a couple hours than the previous twenty-plus years. He's found love and is looking forward to hunkering down for some serious alone time with her.

—I can't imagine a better way for the world to end, he says, then orders another round of shots.

Regulars who I only know within these four walls ask me for my number so we can get together while the bar is closed. I doubt they'll call, but I'm touched they think enough of me to want to spend time together outside our transactional relationship at the Albatross. The thought really *is* the thing that counts.

By the time I kick the last of the stragglers out, there's a pile of bills next to the register that rivals a holiday shift. It's a nice send-off but perhaps it's for good. Who knows how long this thing lasts and if Lon can reopen when the time comes. He runs the place on a shoestring, and his accounting practices would horrify anyone in the square world. Put it this way: the ink ran out in the register before I was hired and he has yet to replace it. I push the buttons on the machine out of habit, but it's mostly ceremonial sense-memory. There's no hard record of drink sales aside from what's in the drawer. But none of the bartenders at the Albatross start with a set bank and Lon dips into it for whatever he needs or wants to buy, be it for the bar or for himself. The garage out back is full of things he paid for from the drawer.

I lock up and walk home wondering if I'll see the inside of the Albatross ever again.

Last Call

The end comes quick. Rose has been getting increasingly frail, but nobody expected her to be gone so soon. Lon takes her to the hospital with some infection and the next thing we know he's making funeral plans.

No one says whether the virus got her or it was something else. Nobody asks.

There's a wake at a parlor a few blocks away. When I show up, the room is full of regulars. Weird to see them in their church clothes rather than on barstools in their customary spots. Lon and his brother greet everyone who arrives.

I don't go to the cemetery, but Lon says he'll be in touch. Says he'll keep me in mind. Weeks pass. Months. The bar (and everything else) remains closed, so I don't think to reach out. Then one day I walk by the bar and the door is open, neon on. I go inside and see a young woman behind the bar who I've never seen before. She cards me, not knowing who I am. I introduce myself. She says she thought Lon was the only bartender. I ask where Lon is, and she says he's out running errands. Said he'd be back in an hour. That was four hours ago.

I leave, ask her to tell him I stopped by. Over the next days I text and call Lon repeatedly. He rarely answers. He's vague and noncommittal. I come back on a night I know he'll be there and ask him to come outside to have a talk.

I ask straight out if he doesn't want me to work at the Albatross anymore. He won't say one way or the other. Says he's keeping me in mind. As if I'm someone off the street who dropped off an application. The years cleaning, mopping, organizing, and pouring drinks are wiped away. As if they never happened.

I don't know what to say to him. It's like going to sleep in one town and waking up in another. I don't know anyone in this new place, though the streets all have the same names and my old friends look and sound like they always did. Lon waves a sheepish farewell and goes back inside. I stand there a minute, then walk down the street to the coffeeshop, wondering whether it will be staffed by pod people as well.

I stop in to the Albatross a couple more times. My list of drink prices is still on the wall above the register, the paintings I've given Lon are still up, a few of the regulars acknowledge my presence, but otherwise I feel like a stranger. Lon tells me he's going to clean out his mom's old rooms but doesn't include me in this plan, nor does he mention anything about bar shifts. I'm out of a job and have no idea why. I think back to when Sharon hired me at the Blue Light without saying a word about it. This is the bizarro world version of that.

His mom's death changes Lon. He's come unmoored, as if she was the last thing keeping him tethered. The bar is shuttered for days at a time now. Sometimes Lon is at the coffeeshop feverishly scribbling away at a drawing. I can tell by the look of him he hasn't slept in days. The girl behind the bar that first day after he reopened is there all the time now. Turns out she's the girlfriend of a guy down the street who gave Lon an art show in his loft/studio. I stop coming in.

These days I make sure to walk on the other side of the street. I look straight ahead when passing by so as not to catch the eye of the smokers outside anymore. I waved to them for the first few weeks, but now it feels forced. I don't go to places I'm not welcome, nor do I want to be reminded of what was, or what could or should have been.

I still live around the corner, so there's no avoiding the place altogether. Not like the Blue Light, which is across town. Still, I see the neighborhood changing. Nothing drastic like an overpass being demolished but small, incremental signs. Strange new businesses are popping up: a prenatal photo studio, a sorority clothing shop. What research did the founders of these places do to warrant them opening here? Who are their clientele? Are they just fronts for something else? Would any of them want to drink at the Albatross? Time will tell.

I can see the wreckers coming. It's just a matter of time. The newcomers to the neighborhood want Starbucks and dry cleaners and health clubs. They will visit a cash-only corner bar on a lark once or twice, as an ironic team-building exercise maybe, but they will never think of it as a place to meet their friends week after week, year after year. The Albatross belongs in the past, to people who are becoming extinct. Soon, it will only live on in stories. In books, if they continue printing books, or in paintings. But who will bother to take the time to look?

I don't mourn the Blue Light because it wasn't mine to lose. I was an interloper there, an outsider even while pouring the drinks. I never belonged there and never tried to. The regulars tried to make friends the best they could, but I never let them close. It was a job in a foreign country. The Albatross is different. It got to me. There were even moments when I felt part of whatever that bar was.

I won't chain myself to the door when the wreckers come, but I'll miss it when it's gone. It's no use trying to live in the past. No use pretending it didn't happen or didn't matter though. It'll never be how it used to be again. It was never the way we remember it. Not as good, not as bad, not as important. Everything and everyone has their time. When we believe we were at our best, our most beautiful.

We return to places like the Albatross to catch a whiff of that feeling. If the pictures on the walls and the drinkers on the barstools remain the same, we can squint and fool ourselves into forgetting the intervening years. But the frequent trips to piss and complaints about aches and pains snap us back into today. When the conversation lulls and we wipe our eyes, we know the glory days weren't so glorious. But gathering with old friends and pretending otherwise is all we have.

When the Albatross is gone, we'll gather at some other bar. We'll huddle together to reminisce. Through our words the old bar will live on, its walls brighter, the patrons more beautiful. We have to believe our lies because the truth can be so ugly, so unbearable.

So, here's to the lies that keep us going.

... Slander

This is my first book to go paperback. Granted, I published the hardcover and signed and numbered all 800-plus copies myself. Who knows if anyone really needs any more? Guess you'll let me know. If you have the hardcover, there's an extra story in this edition just for you...

There's no such bar as the Albatross and no longer a Blue Light as I knew it, but much of what I write about happened in bars that were (and will, perhaps, continue to be) all too real.

If you read this book and believe I'm writing about you, you're right. I am. I changed your name, made you younger but uglier. Combined things you did and said with the words and deeds of others. I couldn't help it. You're always on my mind. If you're offended, motherfuck me to the heavens in your next song/movie/picture/poem. I can't wait to take it the wrong way!

If you own the copyright to Old Style, please don't sue me. I used the name with affection and no intent to sully your brand. Maybe my book will even sell an extra 24-pack or three. No such thing as bad publicity, right?

—*Dmitry Samarov, Chicago, 12/5/25*

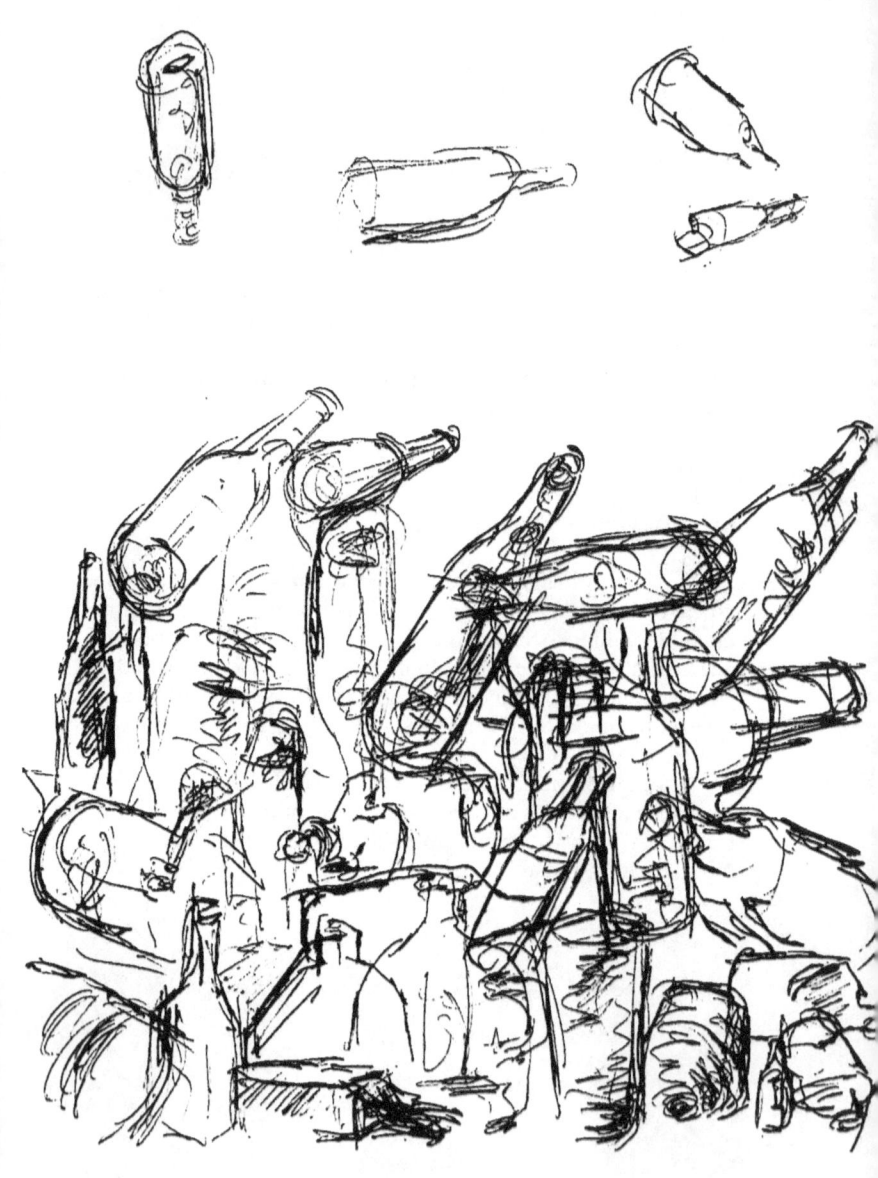